D0960690

THE
NIGHTMARE
THIEF

Nicole Lesperance

TETON COUNTY LIBRARY
JACKSON, WYOMING

sourcebooks
young readers

Copyright © 2021 by Nicole Lesperance
Cover and internal design © 2021 by Sourcebooks
Front cover design by Jordan Kost/Sourcebooks
Jacket design by Allison Sundstrom/Sourcebooks
Cover and internal illustrations © Sourcebooks
Cover illustration and internal illustrations by Federica Frenna
Internal design by Danielle McNaughton/Sourcebooks

Sourcebooks and the colophon are registered trademarks of Sourcebooks.

All rights reserved. No part of this book may be reproduced in any form or by any
electronic or mechanical means including information storage and retrieval systems—
except in the case of brief quotations embodied in critical articles or reviews—without
permission in writing from its publisher, Sourcebooks.

The characters and events portrayed in this book are fictitious or are used fictitiously.
Any similarity to real persons, living or dead, is purely coincidental and not intended by
the author.

Published by Sourcebooks Young Readers, an imprint of Sourcebooks Kids
P.O. Box 4410, Naperville, Illinois 60567-4410
(630) 961-3900
sourcebookskids.com

Library of Congress Cataloging-in-Publication Data

Names: Lesperance, Nicole, author.
Title: The nightmare thief / Nicole Lesperance.
Description: Naperville, Illinois : Sourcebooks Young Readers, [2021] |
    Series: The nightmare thief ; 1 | Audience: Ages 8. | Audience: Grades
    4-6. | Summary: When Maren breaks the strict rules of her family's dream
    shop to help her comatose sister, she is caught and blackmailed by a
    woman with evil plans for the town of Rockpool Bay.
Identifiers: LCCN 2020034485 | (hardcover) | (epub)
Subjects: CYAC: Dreams--Fiction. | Nightmares--Fiction. | Coma--Fiction. |
    Family life--Fiction. | Family-owned business enterprises--Fiction.
Classification: LCC PZ7.1.L4732 Nig 2021 | DDC [Fic]--dc23
LC record available at https://lccn.loc.gov/2020034485

Source of Production: Sheridan Books, Chelsea, Michigan, United States
Date of Production: November 2020
Run Number: 5019704

Printed and bound in the United States of America.
SB 10 9 8 7 6 5 4 3 2 1

For Isla and Neil. Thanks for the disco donuts!

One

MAREN PARTRIDGE WONDERED WHAT HER sister dreamed about. She wondered if people in comas even had dreams. And she wondered if she'd ever find the perfect present for Hallie, who'd lain in a hospital bed for weeks, fast asleep like some sad fairy-tale princess. The fact that it was Hallie's birthday made the need to find the exact, perfect thing so intense that Maren had cracked under the pressure. She'd visited every store in her seaside town, walked every inch of the rocky beach, searched every website she could think of. But none of the presents were right.

A pair of extra-fluffy fleece pajamas.

A set of noise-canceling headphones.

Recordings of herself reading three of Hallie's favorite books, to go along with the headphones.

Ten fresh-out-of-the-package black scented markers. Vanilla, not licorice. The kind Hallie used to carry around in her purse so she could smell them whenever she wanted. The ones that left dark specks on Maren's nose when she stole and sniffed them, instantly giving her away.

Usually Maren had a knack for finding the exact right gift for a person. Not this year, though. Three weeks ago, she'd lost her sister and her knack.

As she dragged her feet along the wooden boards of the town pier, the not-quite-right presents clanked against the tap shoes in her backpack. All around her, lights flashed and jaunty organ music piped. The foamy edges of the waves splashing at the shore were the palest shade of lavender, and the air smelled of salt and, very faintly, cinnamon. No one knew why Rockpool Bay always smelled like baking, even when the bakery was closed. It was just one of the many reasons people traveled miles and miles to vacation there.

"Singing bubbles, five dollars a bottle!" A freckled woman blew a stream of purple bubbles skyward, and the air filled with a shimmering melody. Maren smiled but kept walking. People in comas had no need for bubbles or balloons or riding the world's most rickety roller coaster. Their brains were so badly injured that all they could do was sleep. Nothing could wake them, not bright lights or loud noises or even earthquakes.

It was time to give up. There was nothing here for Hallie.

A little girl shot a rainbow puff of edible fireworks into the sky, and as the fruit-flavored sparkles rained down, she and her brother rushed around, catching them in their mouths. Dodging around the kids, Maren headed down a set of stairs and joined the throngs of sunburnt families on the boardwalk that ran along the waterfront.

A growling rumble announced that the bus was on its way, and she fished four quarters out of her pocket. She had just enough time to make it to her grandmother's dream shop, help for an hour, and get to the hospital. Her mother would meet her there at five thirty, bringing a cake that Hallie couldn't eat.

With a heavy heart, Maren climbed aboard the inky-blue bus, which was dotted with silver stars and golden starfish, and found a seat. The bus lurched forward, turned onto Main Street, then roared and strained up the cobblestone hill that grew steeper and steeper. It inched past the ice cream shop, the grocery store, and the tavern, the crooked structures all leaning on each other for support. The buildings of Rockpool Bay were painted each spring in canary yellow, turquoise, and tulip pink, but as the year wore on, the salty fog stole in and slowly licked the color from their facades.

At the top of the hill, the bus stopped and Maren leapt to

the curb in front of the post office and Mr. Alfredo's Splendid Salon, where everyone always got the perfect haircut. Avoiding the potholes and the puddles that smelled like motor oil and brine, she ducked into the alley between the two buildings.

At the end of the alley, beside a dry cleaner that was almost never open, sat a quiet little shop. The sign over the door said TYPEWRITERS in bold black letters. Tucked in the bottom corner of the window was a sign the size of a business card.

(and dreams), it said in faint cursive.

Fitting her wrought-iron key into the lock, Maren tugged and twisted and pushed. As the door swung open, she inhaled the wonderful scent of ink and paper and musty old machinery. People often stopped to poke their heads inside the shop just long enough to take a whiff of that comforting typewriter smell.

Once her eyes adjusted to the dimness, Maren threaded her way through the jumble of tables. Pastel-colored electric typewriters mingled with ancient manual contraptions whose keys tangled into an impossible clump if you typed on them too fast. In his usual spot beside a Remington Model 5 Streamline lay a gray cat. He opened one eye as Maren approached.

"Hello, Artax." Maren scratched the cat behind his ear, then headed for the narrow door at the back of the room. To a first-time visitor, it would look like someplace only employees were supposed to go—or maybe a bathroom. As Maren turned the brass knob, a croaking screech burst out from the other side.

"GROSSE PATATE."

Maren sighed. "Hello to you, too, Henri."

The room was not, in fact, a storage closet or a bathroom but a space even larger than the typewriter showroom. Shelves and cupboards and drawers rose all the way up to the ceiling. They were crammed with bins and boxes, jars and beakers, measuring cups and spoons. In the corner an old-fashioned silver machine burbled and let out the occasional puff of steam. A rolling ladder had been pushed to one side of the shelves, and on its top rung perched a gray parrot with red tail feathers and a vicious gleam in its beady eyes.

"AVEC UNE FACE DE MARMOTTE." It punctuated the statement with a terrible squawk and began preening its feathers.

"Henri, that's no way to speak to your human-niece. She looks nothing like a potato *or* a marmot." A wrinkly old face appeared from behind the counter in the center of the room. Maren beamed at her grandmother, Lishta, whose hair was the same shade of gray as the parrot's feathers. Today, it was braided and pinned to the top of her head, and she wore a blue dress with an apron tied over it.

"That bird is not my uncle," said Maren. She'd done her

braids just like Lishta's today, except that one of hers was pink and the other green. At four-foot-eleven, Maren was one braid-width taller than her grandmother.

"Given that I adopted him long before you were born," said Lishta, "that technically makes him your uncle." With a cheeky wink, she hurried around the counter and pulled Maren into a hug. Her clothes smelled like lemons, and her body was frail and small-boned, as if she might be the one related to birds. "How are you, my sweet child?"

"Not great," said Maren. "I couldn't find the perfect present for Hallie."

The lines in Lishta's forehead deepened as she sighed. "You've still got time, dear. When she wakes up, you'll have found the perfect thing."

Maren bit the inside of her cheek. She wanted Hallie to wake up *now*, and failing that, she wanted to find the perfect present *now*. "How was Connecticut?"

Lishta sprang back behind the counter where she rummaged, elbow-deep, in an enormous carpeted bag. "Marvelous. Just look at all the ingredients I found." She began pulling objects out and setting them on the counter. Broken crusts of cement; a handful of tiny flags on toothpicks; stoppered vials of various liquids; a tuft of sheep's fleece with twigs tangled in it. Maren tugged on the rolling ladder, which let out a rusty squeak as it trundled along the floor. Henri shuffled and flapped but maintained his perch at the top.

"One-oh-seven," said Lishta, opening a tube of lipstick and scooping out its fuchsia insides. Maren climbed halfway up the ladder and retrieved a purple hatbox with the number 107 stenciled onto its side. She passed it down to Lishta, who dropped the empty tube of lipstick inside and slid the lid back on. It still felt strange, working at the dream shop without Hallie or her mother. But her mother had switched from part-time to full-time at her office job to help cover Hallie's medical bills and had no time to help at the shop anymore.

"What next?" said Maren.

Lost in contemplation, Lishta rubbed her thumb over the lid of a faded metal tin that had once held breath mints. Her lips moved silently.

"Gran-Gran?" Maren stepped onto the lowest rung of the ladder and shoved off, rumbling toward the old woman. Just before they collided, Maren hopped off. Lishta jolted and almost dropped the tin.

"What number?" said Maren, reaching for the silver box.

Lishta set the tin on the counter and pulled a hairpin from one of her braids. She stuck the pin between her teeth, set her hands on her hips, and stared at the tin as though expecting it to do something. Maren wasn't sure what.

"What's in there?" said Maren.

"Whispering dust," said Lishta. "I've been searching for the stuff for years."

She broke off as the handle of the door leading back into the showroom jiggled and squeaked. It turned halfway, then stopped. On the other side, Artax meowed, and a man's voice murmured.

"It's open," called Lishta, scooping up the tin and tucking it into her apron pocket. "Please do come in."

The door opened a crack and Artax slipped through, triggering a string of French profanities from Henri. Flapping her hands at the bird, Lishta crossed the room and pulled open the door, revealing a short, startled, bald man.

"I'm sorry," he said, fiddling with the button on his tweed jacket. "It's just... Well, this sounds ridiculous, but it seemed like the cat wanted me to let it in here, or maybe it..."

With an encouraging nod, Lishta clasped her hands behind her back and waited.

"It wanted me to come in." The man's voice dropped to a whisper. He cast an apologetic smile at Maren, who returned the expression and busied herself with tidying up the scattered spools of thread on the counter. Hallie always threw them in the sewing box in a tangled mess, but Maren liked to keep them neat.

"Perhaps he did," said Lishta, scratching Artax's back as he wove around her ankles.

The man coughed and blinked, staring up at the towering shelves. "Is it really true?" he whispered. "That you sell dreams?"

"It is, indeed." Beaming, Lishta took the man's elbow and led him to the counter. "What are you looking for, my dear?"

"I'm not sure." The man didn't seem to know what to do with his hands; he stuffed them in his pockets and yanked them out again. "How does it work?"

Maren tucked the last spool of thread into the sewing box and stowed it away under the counter. She opened a wide-mouthed jar and slid it over to Lishta, who reached inside and pulled out a handful of pale pink packets. They looked like tea bags but were the size of buttons.

"We craft them ourselves," said Lishta, holding out the sachets. The man picked one up cautiously and sniffed it. "Everything is hand-collected, portioned, mixed, and ground." Lishta gestured at the coffee grinder on the counter, an ancient contraption with a hand crank on the top and a little red drawer in its base. "And sterilized, of course." She pointed to the silver machine in the corner, which let out a burp of steam. "We've got hundreds of premade dreams, but we can craft anything you like."

"I wouldn't know where to start." The man held the sachet up to the light to inspect its hand-sewn edge.

The door swung open again, and a tall woman strode in. Her dark hair swirled behind her, and she wore a slash of deep-plum lipstick. She slapped her purse onto the counter beside the bald man, who jumped and dropped the dream sachet he'd been looking at.

"We'll be right with you, madam," said Lishta. The woman gave her a curt nod and picked a thread off her cardigan. On her collar, she'd pinned a brooch in the shape of a snow-white moth.

"JOLIE MADEMOISELLE. BONJOUR, BONJOUR, CHERIE." Henri flapped down to the counter beside the woman. Maren had purposely chosen to take Spanish instead of French at school because it was better not to understand what Henri said. But she was fairly sure "jolie" meant *pretty*, but she had never heard Henri say anything nice about anyone besides Lishta. He sidled up to the woman's purse, and then Maren understood. The clasp was shaped like a safety pin. Henri was obsessed with safety pins.

"That dream you're holding is one of our most popular," said Lishta to the bald man. "It's a flying dream. Our customers often tell us the euphoria lasted the whole next day. Sometimes two or three days."

Maren nodded along as Lishta spoke, feeling the dark-haired woman's steely gaze on her. Customers generally didn't want to hear a sales pitch from a twelve-year-old, but Lishta said her presence made them more trusting. And this year, Lishta had finally started teaching her how to create her own dreams.

"Our dreams can help with all kinds of ailments, physical and psychological," said Lishta. "High blood pressure, gout, thyroid conditions, lovesickness." She gave the man an appraising look. "Anxiety, perhaps?" He nodded nervously, and Lishta pulled out a wooden box filled with green sachets. Maren had helped her mother craft this batch of calming dreams: powdered midsummer raindrops, the softest edges of goose-down feathers, a scratching of fresh nutmeg, and a tiny snip from the lining of a brand-new pencil box.

"How do I take this?" The man handed the pink sachet back to Lishta. Beside him, the tall woman let out an irritated *tsk* and ruffled the feathers on Henri's chest. Maren couldn't believe he didn't snap at her finger.

Lishta selected three fresh green dreams from the box and tucked them inside a plastic pouch. "Place one of these under your tongue when you get into bed," she said. "You won't even notice it, I assure you. The mesh will dissolve as you sleep, and there won't be any trace when you wake up. Just make sure not to get it wet before then."

Lishta's Canadian cousin hand-wove the dream sachets and mailed them to her in giant boxes. Maren wasn't sure exactly what they were made out of, but they were designed to let the dream leak out as soon as moisture touched them. You had to be very careful about keeping the dreams dry—especially the nightmares, which let out a nauseating smell when they were released and could seep through a person's skin and give them terrible hallucinations, even if they were awake.

The man nodded eagerly and took out his wallet, but Lishta held up a finger. Maren ducked under the counter and pulled out a sheet of paper with the dream contract printed on it.

"We have one key rule," said Lishta, and, although this was all part of the usual spiel, Maren's chest warmed, as it always did, at the word "we." At the fact that it was *her* rule, too. "You must agree to the rule and sign this contract before we can sell you the dream."

The tall woman sighed again and made a show of checking her watch, but Lishta ignored her. Following her lead, Maren gave the man the kind, yet serious expression she'd been working on all summer, and slid the contract across the counter.

"This dream is only for your personal consumption." Lishta pulled on a pair of wire-framed glasses and switched from her kind voice to her stern, rules-following one. "You must promise never to give it to anyone else without their consent. The subconscious brain is a fragile and easily influenced thing. No person should ever take or be given a dream he or she does not understand or expect, and no dream should ever be given with the intent of influencing another person's thoughts, fears, hopes, memories, or wishes." Lishta peered over her glasses. "Is that clear?"

"Perfectly," said the dark-haired woman, though nobody was speaking to her. She rolled her eyes at Maren, who pretended not to notice.

"If we find out that you've broken this rule, the next time you come to the shop, the door will be locked," said Lishta to the nervous man. "And the next time, and the next. There are no second chances. You're banned for life."

The first time she'd ever taken a dream, Maren had signed a copy of this contract, too, and Lishta had been very clear that she'd face the same consequence if she broke the rule. But as she listened to her grandmother recite her speech for the thousandth time, a seed of an idea sprouted in Maren's head.

A birthday-present-shaped seed.

Even more than a birthday present. If dreams could cure all kinds of ailments, why not a brain injury? Maybe there was a way to fix Hallie that the doctors hadn't thought of. Maybe it was worth breaking the rule if it meant getting her sister back.

Maren's feet began quietly tapping the steps for her upcoming dance recital.

Step toe toe heel step shuffle ball change.

The bald man picked up a pen. "Is that it?"

"That is it," said Lishta. "Do you solemnly swear?"

"I do." He printed out his name and address in tiny, meticulous writing, then signed the bottom of the page while Lishta wrapped up his dreams in a square of brown paper. As the man slowly counted his change and pocketed his wallet and the paper parcel, the dark-haired woman let out a loud huff. She drummed her long fingernails on the counter until he was gone.

"Now, the jolie mademoiselle," said Lishta, closing the lid of the wooden box. "How may I help you?"

The woman's mouth stretched into an oily grin. "Give me a dozen of your worst nightmares."

Two

Lᴉsʜᴛᴀ sʟᴉᴅ ᴛʜᴇ ʙᴏx ᴏғ calming dreams over to Maren and folded her arms across her narrow chest. "Ms.…Malo, is it?"

The dark-haired woman hesitated for a flicker of an instant. "Yes, that's right." She tugged her cardigan around her slender waist, and the moth on the collar opened and closed its wings. It wasn't a brooch; it was a real insect.

"How do you get it to stay there?" Lishta eyed the moth with keen interest, and so did Henri. The fuzzy-bodied creature would make a perfect addition to some dream—once it died of natural causes, of course. Lishta would never kill something just for that purpose.

The woman smiled down at the moth, which extended its long antennae and crawled up to nestle against her collarbone. "I have a…certain way with winged insects, you might say."

Her dark eyes flashed to Lishta's, and the two women held each other's gaze.

There was something in the lavender-edged waters of Rockpool Bay, people said, or maybe the town had been settled by fairy folk or witches a long time ago. Whatever it was, like in other pockets of the world, a small percentage of its residents were born with very specific, small magic. Maren's family on her mother's side had dream magic, from Lishta to Maren's mother to Hallie and Maren. If anyone else tried grinding up ingredients and putting them in a sachet, nothing would happen. When the women of Maren's family did that and then blew on the ingredients, they made dreams.

Other people had different kinds of small magic. If you went to the post office and bought a certain stamp from the vending machine and gave it to Edna Frye, the crotchety postmistress, your letter or package would arrive at its destination the very same day, regardless of where in the world you sent it. At the Green and Fresh grocery store, a massive yellow rosebush sprouted out of the floor, right in the middle of the produce aisle. The owner, Ernesto Perez, kept it well pruned so the thorns wouldn't scratch any customers. On Thursdays he handed out free roses to anyone who wanted them, and on Fridays they all grew back.

Maren had never heard of magic that let people

communicate with insects, though. Lishta seemed equally fascinated. The old woman gazed at the moth for a long while, then blinked rapidly as if to clear her head. She readjusted her apron.

"I'm afraid I can't sell you more than three nightmares at a time. If you read the fine print of the contract you signed a few months ago, you'll see that it's spelled out quite clearly."

Maren's fingers slid toward the pink flying dream that lay forgotten on the counter. She had taken one last week, and it was everything Lishta had promised it'd be. When she closed her eyes, Maren could still feel the effortless weight-lessness, the chilly wind kissing her face. It was the perfect sensation for someone trapped in a hospital bed. The perfect dream to energize somebody, to enliven them and give them the strength to heal and wake up.

Shuffle ball change stamp went Maren's feet. Hallie would never tell on her for breaking the rule, even if she woke up tomorrow. Her fingernail scratched the stitched edge of the pink sachet.

"How about five?" said the woman.

Lishta shook her head. "You signed the contract agree-ing to our terms. If you'd like to take your business elsewhere, that's fine."

Maren's lips twitched with a barely suppressed grin. This

was the only dream shop on the entire East Coast. Maren's distant cousins in Oklahoma also had dream magic, but they didn't make nightmares. There were rumors of other shops hidden around Europe and the Middle East, but Maren knew nothing about them.

"Four, then." The woman opened her handbag. "I'll pay you double for them."

"It's three or nothing," said Lishta. "Rules are rules, and I refuse to haggle."

Before her grandmother noticed the stray dream on the counter, Maren tucked it inside her fist.

"VOLEUSE!" shouted Henri. The tall woman glanced sharply at Maren, who felt her face go hot.

"No one is stealing anything," said Lishta. "Ms. Malo will pay for her nightmares, just like everyone else."

Pulse thundering, Maren turned away and pretended to put the dream in a jar, sliding it inside her sleeve instead. Busy wheeling the ladder over to the opposite side of the shelves, Lishta didn't notice.

"If I'm only getting three, they'd better be terrifying," snapped the dark-haired woman.

Lishta's shoulders hunched up for a second. "I'm certain I have the perfect thing for you, dear." As she climbed the ladder, Henri fluttered up to the top rung, then hopped impatiently from one side to the other until she reached him. With a happy squawk, he leapt on top of the old woman's head and settled comfortably on her braids.

Maren never understood why people bought nightmares on purpose. Lishta said it was the same reason some people loved horror movies, except dreams were even more vivid and immersive. Nightmares were like being *in* a horror movie. They made people's hearts gallop, chilled their bones, and made them feel alive. Once it ended, once their drumming pulse slowed and they found themselves back in their safe, mundane lives, they appreciated everything so much more. Halloween was always the busiest time of year for the dream shop, with even the most sensible customers looking to scare themselves silly.

Maren hated too-scary Halloween things and horror movies, and she couldn't stand the nightmares her brain cooked up all on its own. She couldn't imagine doing that to herself on purpose. But Hallie was a huge nightmare fan. She was always making new ones and trying to convince Maren to take them, but Maren would rather shove worms up her nose than have bad dreams. Hallie had even made a few nightmares that Lishta deemed too horrible to sell in the shop, which Hallie saw as the ultimate compliment.

"Let me see," said Lishta, unlocking the nightmare cabinet

and rummaging through the boxes and jars inside. "Three of our ripest nightmares to terrify and delight the jolie mademoiselle."

"JOLIE JOLIE!" echoed Henri.

But instead of choosing something from the jet-black jars and tins, Lishta selected a gray cardboard box. These were what she called training nightmares, designed for new customers to make sure they were tough enough to handle the really scary ones. Lishta gave the box a loud sniff and swung backward on the ladder, rolling her eyes dramatically. Henri flapped and croaked, but kept hold of her braids.

"I'd almost forgotten about these beauties," she said. The dark-haired woman's eyes gleamed as Lishta made a show of selecting three nightmares and then locked the box away again.

"What are they?" said the woman.

"An ancient Egyptian pyramid." Lishta climbed creakily down the ladder with Henri still on her head. "You're trapped inside, running down a dark passage." Her voice lowered. "Down, down into the bowels of the earth you go, dank and rotting and festering. And then you find a massive black sarcophagus covered in cobwebs."

The woman let out a delighted gasp, and Lishta paused. "I don't want to ruin the whole thing for you, dear."

The woman blinked for a moment. "Yes. Yes, of course." She pulled out her wallet. "How much for them?"

"Twenty-one dollars," said Lishta. What she'd neglected to mention about the nightmare was that once the sarcophagus was opened, it contained a giant teddy bear.

As the woman counted out her money, Maren transferred the dream from her sleeve to her pocket. Hallie loved the Egyptian tomb dream, even though it wasn't very frightening. Unfortunately, Lishta always kept the nightmares locked up, and stealing one would be nearly impossible. Anyway, it wasn't right to give somebody a nightmare without their consent, even if it was just a training nightmare.

Guilt nibbled at Maren's skin. Giving Hallie any kind of dreams without her consent meant messing with her subconscious.

Hop shuffle step, hop shuffle step, shuff—

"Sweetheart?" Lishta's curious eyes blinked, inches from Maren's nose. Maren let out a tiny squeak and leapt backward.

"ELLE A LA TETE DANS LES NUAGES!" screeched Henri from his ladder perch. The tall woman was gone.

"Hadn't you better get going?" said Lishta.

One of the clocks on one of the lower shelves read five twenty. Another read five forty, which meant it was somewhere around five thirty. Maren's gaze strayed to the jar of flying dreams. It wasn't wrong to want to cure her sister. If this worked, they'd see that she was right and all would be forgiven.

"Would you like a few of those for yourself?" said Lishta. "They might cheer you up, and we can make another batch later this week."

"Thank you," Maren said, slipping two more dreams into her pocket and feeling even guiltier now that Lishta had gifted her the exact thing she'd stolen.

"Give your sister one of these, and tell her happy birthday," said Lishta, and Maren flinched before realizing she had blown two kisses at her and she was meant to give one of *those* to Hallie. Lishta wasn't giving her permission to give Hallie a dream. That would never happen.

Maren shouldered her bag and headed for the door. She imagined the dreams dissolving, ripping a hole in her jeans, and shouting her secret out through it, though of course they could never do that. As Maren cast one last glance over her shoulder, Lishta opened the combination safe where she kept the money and set the tin of whispering dust all the way in the back.

Three

MAREN RACED THROUGH THE ALLEY, leaping puddles and dodging cracks. In the street ahead, a heavy engine grumbled. The bus. If she missed this one, she'd never make it to the hospital in time. Pumping her legs harder, she skidded around the corner. Suddenly, the post office door swung open. Maren threw her arms out, ricocheted off the glass pane, and tumbled to the cobblestones.

"Are you all right?" A boy's voice, one she'd rather not have heard, but there was no time to react. The bus was already at the stop, and the doors were going to shut any moment now. Maren shoved away the hand trying to help her up and staggered to her feet.

"Wait!" she yelled, ignoring the bite of pain in her knee and sprinting for the bus stop. "Wait!"

The closing door of the star/starfish bus swung back open, and with a gasp of relief Maren threw herself up the steps. She fished four quarters out of her pocket, making sure not to drop the dream sachets.

"Everybody move down," called the bus driver, and Maren stuffed herself into the jumble of passengers filling the aisle. As the bus lurched forward, everyone wobbled and swayed, and Maren caught hold of a greasy handle on the back of a seat. Somebody smelled like tacos, and somebody else was listening to bluegrass music loud enough for the whole bus to hear. In the seat next to Maren, a middle-aged woman sat knitting a baby sweater that kept changing colors.

"Sorry I hit you," said the same boy's voice. Maren was wedged too tightly to turn and look at him, but she didn't need to. It was Amos O'Grady, the curly-haired boy who used to be her best friend—before he started hanging out with kids who made up nasty stories about people and ruined their lives.

"Don't worry about it." Maren worked her bag around to the front of her body and slid out a paperback book. She only had enough space to hold the book inches from her nose, too close to actually read the words, but it didn't matter as long as it made Amos stop talking. Her knee still stung, and she felt blood trickling down her shin.

The bus rumbled past Maisie Mae's Frozen Delights,

with its usual line of customers stretching down the sidewalk. Maisie's ice cream magic was similar to Maren's dream magic, in that it influenced people's minds, but on a smaller scale. Each flavor put her customers in a different mood. Peppermint gave them the elated feeling of the last day of school, bubble-gum caused uncontrollable giggles, and lemon-rosemary sorbet dredged up long-forgotten memories. Spicy chocolate cayenne was a mixed bag. Sometimes it warmed people up on a cold day, but sometimes it started unnecessary fights.

At the waterfront, most of the passengers got off and headed for the pier. For half a minute, the air filled with sunshine and cinnamon and the carefree lightness of people on vacation. Then the doors swung shut, and the bus was quiet. Maren found a sideways-facing seat near the front, where she tucked her knees up, made a barrier with her book, and pretended not to notice Amos, now wedged in beside the knitting woman with the color-changing sweater. He wore a blue soccer jersey—he was the middle school team's goalie—and every time Maren looked up, his eyes darted away.

The buildings grew wider, browner, and more purposeful as they left the touristy part of town. Maren pushed the button for the next stop, and when the bus juddered to a halt in front of the hulking brick hospital, she leapt out.

Amos got out right behind her. Maren stuffed her book

into her bag and jogged toward the entrance. The glass doors hushed open, letting out a gust of disinfectant and floor wax. Trying to ignore the instant wave of sadness it gave her, Maren slowed her jog to a speed-walk. The hospital, like the police station and the registry of motor vehicles, was a magic-free building. Here they believed in the power of science, of things that could be measured and tested and proven. Not flighty, unpredictable things like magic.

Amos stopped at the reception desk, which gave Maren a head start to dive into the elevator and stab at the number five button until the doors closed. The elevator shot upward, leaving her stomach somewhere down near the first floor. In these last moments of silence, she always worried that something terrible had happened to Hallie and nobody had remembered to get in touch with her. Even after three weeks of nothing more terrible than her sister still being uncon-scious, the fear was always the worst in the elevator, the vivid visions of Hallie about to die or dead, of finding just an empty bed.

Mom would've called if anything happened, Maren told herself. *Hallie is fine. YOU are fine.*

Fine fine fine fine squeaked her sneakers as she walked down the spotless hallway of the children's ward. The walls were covered in murals of balloons and animals and fairy castles, but their brightness seemed like a joke nobody was laughing at.

Flower arrangements in various stages of dying filled Hallie's room. People had been bringing them in every day since the accident, and Maren wished they would stop. Hallie couldn't see the flowers, and they made her room smell like a funeral.

In her bed, Hallie lay like a doll with the covers folded in a straight line across her torso. She used to sleep like a hurricane, blankets tumbled, legs askew, pillows on the floor. Now she looked too neat, too orderly, too...organized. Her cheeks were hollow, her blond hair dull and limp. Wires connected her to various machines, one bag feeding nutrients into her arm and another collecting what came back out. Maren fought the urge to imagine she'd wandered into the wrong room. There was no use pretending this was someone else: she had a trio of freckles over her left eyebrow and a scar on her arm from falling out of a go-cart when she was nine and Maren was five.

"Happy birthday, big sis," said Maren, piling all of her not-right presents at the foot of the bed. "How are you?"

Hallie never answered, but Maren always gave her a little time, just in case. She swallowed a twinge of disappointment and pulled the uncomfortable brown chair close to the bed. Then she uncapped a marker and held it under Hallie's nose, careful not to get any black spots on her.

Still nothing. Maren gave the marker a deep, vanilla sniff, then capped it with a sigh. "Gran-Gran's back from Connecticut. She got a whole bunch of new stuff. And there's this special kind of dust that she"—Maren leaned in close to whisper—"put in the safe. What do you think it's for?"

Again, Hallie showed no sign of responding, of hearing, of existing in the waking world, but Maren pressed on anyway.

"I bet it does something really cool. Something even better than falling in love or snuggling a pile of puppies or flying." Her hand strayed to her pocket, but footsteps squeaked down the hallway. Two nurses stopped to chat outside Hallie's room, and Maren slumped back in her chair.

"I saw that worm Amos on the bus here," she said. "Remember what a crush he used to have on you?" She couldn't help grinning at the memory of eight-year-old Amos leaving bouquets of dandelions and buttercups on their doorstep. Of the time she told him Hallie's favorite poet was Emily Dickinson, so he'd gone to the library, made a photocopy of "'Why do I love' You, Sir?" and then crossed out "Sir" and "Sire" and written in "Madam" and "Ma'am." Hallie and Maren had laughed for weeks. Even now—well, until the accident—one of them only had to say "Madam?" in a snooty English accent and they'd both collapse into snorting hysterics.

Maren tried it now, but no one laughed. She reached for her pocket again, but just then the door swung open and her mother's pinched face appeared.

"Oh good, you're here," she said, though she looked at Hallie as she said it. She set a store-bought cake on the table beside the bed but didn't remove its plastic cover.

"Where's Dad?" asked Maren.

"Working late." Her mom rubbed her eyes, which were always red around the edges now. "He already came by on his lunch break."

Maren's dad had been picking up a lot of extra shifts recently. At night in bed, Maren heard her parents talking in hushed, worried tones about Hallie's medical bills.

"Have you ever wondered what might happen if we gave her a dream?" Maren meant to sound nonchalant, but she couldn't keep the raw longing out of her voice.

Shuffle heel step heel...

"Maren Eloise." Somehow her mother sounded even more tired than before, like she hadn't slept in a thousand years. "Your sister's poor brain needs to rest so that it can heal. And it's against hospital policy. You know better."

Maren did know better. But it seemed like nobody was trying to *do* anything to help Hallie, and she couldn't stand waiting any longer. "Should we sing to her?" she said, before she had a chance to blurt out any other incriminating things.

Maren's mom glanced at the cake and sighed. "I suppose we should."

A gentle rap sounded on the door, and one of Hallie's dozens of doctors poked her head inside. "Is this a good time?"

"Of course," said Maren's mom.

The doctor gave Maren a little wave, then turned to her mom. "I have the brochures for those long-term-care facilities."

Long-term care didn't mean days or weeks. It was an impossible, never-ending amount of time to wait. If Hallie didn't wake up by next Thursday—ten days from now—she had to move to one of those places where they didn't expect anybody to get better anytime soon. And their insurance wasn't going to cover it. Maren's throat felt lumpy, like it was full of wet papier-mâché.

"I'll be right back," she said.

A rainbow unicorn grinned down at her from the hallway wall, and Maren wanted to punch its ridiculous, toothy mouth. She found the drinking fountain and gulped and gulped its metallic water, not stopping to breathe until the world began to swim.

"Leave some for the rest of us," came a woman's sharp voice. Usually people said that as a joke, but this person sounded like she really thought Maren was going to drink all the water in the hospital. Wiping her mouth, Maren turned and was surprised to see the woman who'd been in the dream shop earlier. Ms. Malo. She held a drooping, brown plant in a pot, and the white moth perched on her shoulder with its wings folded down.

"Oh…uh, hello," said Maren.

Showing no sign of recognizing Maren, the woman nudged past and drank deeply from the water fountain, but gave none to her parched plant. She wiped her purple mouth on her sleeve, but the lipstick didn't budge. Without making eye contact, she turned and clacked away to the double doors at the end of the hall.

"You should put her in the Sterling Center," she said without looking back.

Maren's mouth dropped open. "Were you listening to us?"

The door swung shut. Bewildered, Maren headed back toward Hallie's room.

"I'll talk to Scott tonight." Her mother and the doctor emerged. "Thank you again. Maren, I'm just going to use the restroom and then we'll have our cake."

The last thing Maren wanted was cake, but she was glad for the time alone with Hallie. As casually as she could, she pushed the door almost all the way shut, leaving just a tiny gap so she could hear her mother coming back. She tiptoed to Hallie's bed.

"Happy birthday to you," whisper-sang Maren. She leaned over like she was kissing her sister's hollow cheek and carefully opened her mouth. "Happy birthday to you." Hallie's tongue felt rubbery like a doll's, and Maren wondered if the dream would dissolve properly, if it might accidentally choke her sister, but as soon as the sachet touched Hallie's tongue, it began to disintegrate.

"Happy birthday, dear Hallie."

Footsteps squeaked down the hall, and Maren heard the distinctive jingle of her mom's keys. She backed away from the bed, sat in the chair, and watched her sister's face.

"Happy birthday to you," she finished. Only a few wisps of white and pink remained where the sachet had been, and the tiniest trace of a smile had appeared on Hallie's lips.

Four

"Mom, she was snooping around and listening to private medical conversations." Maren slid into the back seat of her mother's car and tugged her seat belt so tight that it cut into her neck. Even though the accident happened weeks ago, Maren still felt extremely nervous in cars. "There are *laws* against that. Don't you even care?"

Her mom sighed. It felt like the only thing she ever did these days, like she had too much bad air inside her now that Hallie was broken and she had to keep letting it out. "It's not that I don't care. It's just that it's probably not worth getting so upset over."

"But the fact that she was just in the dream shop this afternoon, plus that?" said Maren. "It seems very strange."

"It's a little strange, yes." Maren's mother checked her

rearview mirror, then each side mirror, then the rearview again, then shifted the car into reverse. "But we can't exactly call the police to complain about somebody being in the same place as you twice in one day."

"And spying on me." Maren tugged her seat belt a little tighter.

Another heavy sigh. "If you see her again, we'll talk. Okay?"

Maren slumped as they inched toward the parking lot exit. She knew she shouldn't add to her family's list of things to worry about. She'd seen the pills her mother took every night before bed. Apparently even Lishta's best dreams couldn't fix her levels of anxiety.

"Do you think you might come to the shop sometime this week?" said Maren. "Maybe one day after work, you and me and Gran-Gran could—"

"Is that Amos?" Maren's mother pointed to the bus stop, where a curly-haired kid sat on the bench, buried in his phone.

"Yes." Maren slouched lower in her seat.

Instead of turning left toward their house, Maren's mom pulled up to the bus stop. She lowered the passenger-side window. "Amos!"

Amos jolted upright. "Hi, Mrs. Par—I mean Julia."

Maren's parents hated formal titles, but Amos always felt

weird calling them by their first names. His cheeks went pink as he peered into the back seat, and Maren wrinkled her nose.

"Can we give you a lift?" said Maren's mother.

"Mom, no!" hissed Maren, but it was too late. Amos had gotten up. He hesitated between opening the front or the back door, then got into the back. Maren whipped her head straight forward. This couldn't be happening. Now she'd have to talk to him.

"Thanks," he said, pulling on his seat belt. "I missed the bus, and my mom's driving Benny to baseball tonight."

"How is your mother?" Maren's mom triple-checked all her mirrors, then crept back onto the street. "I haven't seen her since you guys moved."

"She's good. Just busy."

Amos's parents had gotten divorced last fall. After his dad ran off to Alaska, his mom had moved Amos and his brother from their house on Maren's street to a duplex across town. The move wasn't what had killed Maren's friendship with Amos, not exactly. She'd called him every night and listened to him talk and cry. She'd given him handfuls of dreams to ease his sadness and worries, and she'd even convinced him to see the school therapist. What killed Maren's friendship with Amos was his new neighbor and sudden new best friend, Curtis Mayhew.

"What were you doing in the hospital?" she blurted out. Amos looked surprised she'd actually spoken to him.

"My grandpa's there," he said. "He had a heart attack."

"Oh, that's awful," said Maren. Old Mr. O'Grady used to come to Amos's house on Tuesdays to watch him and his brother. He always invited the whole neighborhood over to play softball in their backyard.

"I'm so sorry," said Maren's mom. "Is he going to be okay?"

"The doctors think so. But nobody else has time to visit him." Amos traced a square on the back of his phone. "He's asleep most of the time, and when he's awake, he doesn't always know who I am."

Maren wondered if a dream might help Amos's grandfather remember him. Brains are stubborn, Lishta had told her. They hold on to things we don't even realize, bury them deep under layers and layers. Lishta had just begun teaching Maren how to make memory dreams. The trick was to find a vivid, import-ant event and then collect ingredients from the place where it happened or someplace very similar. If it happened near a lake, for example, you could scrape wood splinters from the underside of a dock and grind them with fibers from a beach towel and the feather of a loon. The brain would pick up these threads of memory and recraft the scene, doing most of the work itself.

Mr. O'Grady deserved a dream like that, but it didn't

sound like he could consent to it. She couldn't risk breaking the rules for two people, as much as she wished she could.

"Please tell your mom I'm here if she needs anything," said Maren's mother, and Maren wondered how she could possibly help anyone when she could barely keep her own life together. She wondered if at this exact moment, Hallie was dreaming of flying.

Slowly, very slowly, the car turned onto a street lined with identical duplexes, and a kid flashed past on a bike. Maren tucked her knees up and shuddered as he skidded to a stop across the street from the driveway they were about to pull into. It was Curtis, the meanest kid in Maren's grade. He peered inside the car and smirked when he saw Amos in the back seat. Maren hunched so low that she had to loosen her seat belt. She didn't care if it made her unsafe.

Amos glanced across the street and muttered something Maren couldn't hear. "Thanks again," he said as he climbed out of the car. Just before the door swung shut, he locked eyes with Maren and said "Bye." Something resembling a smile flickered across his mouth and disappeared.

Maren's forehead went prickly. If it were possible to sink any lower without lying on the floor, she would have done it. As her mom began cycling through her mirror-checking routine, Curtis called across the street to Amos.

"Go, just go, go, go," Maren whispered. Her mother turned on her headlights, sprayed wiper fluid onto the windshield, and let the wipers run until they screeched on the dry glass. She checked her mirrors one more time. Finally, at the speed of a very old snail, they were off.

Five

Sprawled on the purple velvet couch of her living room, Maren turned on the TV and navigated to her recorded shows. *Dance Like Everybody's Watching* sat at the top of the list. Maren had watched every episode multiple times. She liked episode four best because Imani Epps, the eleven-year-old tap-dancing prodigy from Sacramento, had performed a dazzling solo to one of Maren's favorite songs. Maren selected that episode, set down the remote, and dug her fork into the plastic tray of tasteless pasta her mom had microwaved for dinner.

The music began, a thumping groove that filled the theater. Wearing a sparkling green bodysuit, Imani swung her leg over her head, grabbed her ankle, and spun until she blurred. Leaping out of her spin and flashing the crowd an enormous grin, she launched into a dizzyingly fast combination of tap footwork.

Several times, Maren had tried slowing down the recording and teaching herself the combination, but it proved impossible.

"Whoa, did you see that?" she said, even though she'd watched—and forced her mom to watch—this particular solo twenty times already.

"Hmm?" Maren's mom peered over the top of her glasses.

Maren rewound the show, and Imani catapulted through the routine again. Murmuring appreciatively, her mother returned to the brochure she'd been reading. A half-dozen other pamphlets for long-term facilities lay scattered across the couch. They kept sliding over and pricking Maren's bare foot with their pointy corners, and she kept kicking them back toward her mother.

Maren used to love when her dad worked late. It meant she and Hallie got to watch TV and eat frozen dinners on the couch. Now it meant Maren and her mom ate frozen dinners and the empty house nearly swallowed them up. Shivering, Maren focused on the rest of Imani's solo, hoping the sequins and dazzle would push the shadows out of her brain.

A prickly beard brushed the top of her head, and she yelped. "Dad! I didn't hear you come in."

"That's because I'm stealthy." Maren's dad tiptoed over to the coffee table and spun around, waggling his fingers like a magician.

"Scott!" Maren's mom snatched an antique jar filled with dreams away from her flailing husband. He thumped down onto the sofa and let out a tired groan.

"Did you hear about the Green and Fresh?" he said. "A bunch of angry wasps came swarming out of the rosebush."

Maren shuddered and instinctively looked for her bag, where she kept an EpiPen. Even though she hadn't been stung in years, she remembered the terrifying sensation of her face swelling up, her throat closing in, her breath turning to a thin wheeze. The sickening panic of slowly suffocating.

"A bunch of people got stung," continued her dad. "They ended up having to close the whole store and call an exterminator." He gave Maren a reassuring pat on the knee. "Good thing you weren't in there today, Mare-Bear."

Maren gulped and nodded. She rewound Imani's solo to take her mind off insects like wasps and bees. It seemed deeply unfair that such dainty little creatures—some of which made things as lovely as honey—could potentially kill her.

"You're sitting on the Sterling brochure," said her mom, pulling the pamphlet out from under her husband's leg.

"Please don't send Hallie to Sterling," said Maren. "I don't want that lady knowing where she is." Hopefully there would be no need for Sterling or any other facility once Maren's dreams started curing Hallie, but she didn't want to risk it.

Her mom let out another gust of sad air. "It's one of the best facilities in the area. Maybe she was just trying to help."

Maren was certain she wasn't, though she couldn't say precisely why. It had something to do with the fact that the woman hadn't given her plant any water when it was clearly dying of thirst. The way she pretended not to recognize Maren. The angry sharpness of her voice.

Step toe toe heel step went Maren's bare feet under the coffee table, trying to keep up with lovely, glittering Imani on the screen. Ten days. She still had ten days to cure Hallie.

"It's also the most expensive facility." Maren's dad hefted himself off the couch and headed for the kitchen.

"There's a mac and cheese in the freezer," said Maren's mom. "Sorry I didn't cook, but I did manage to pick up some overtime next week."

The long-term centers were all at least a half hour away and not on the bus line. If both of her parents were working all the time, nobody would be able to drive Maren to visit Hallie. She wished they could bring Hallie home and take care of her themselves—she'd let her have their shared bedroom to herself so all of her machines could fit. Maren would be happy to sleep on the couch. Or the floor. Or outside in a tent.

Maren didn't know where her family would go if they lost their house because of medical bills. Lishta's apartment only had one bedroom. Maybe they'd have to move to Virginia, where her other grandmother lived, but Maren wasn't sure she could stand living in an utterly magicless town. And how would they move Hallie? Could they put her on a plane in her bed? Would they have to fold her into a wheelchair? Would they have to leave her here?

"Gran-Gran's been paying me," said Maren. "You can have that money, too."

Her mom's worried frown softened. "That's very kind, Mare, but you keep it. Use it for school stuff."

Panic zapped through Maren's chest. There were still four days left of July, and she was pretending September didn't exist. She'd lost Amos, and she dreaded going back to that school full of teasing kids alone. Maren turned off the television. She couldn't stomach watching anyone be sparkly and captivating and perfect anymore.

"I'm going to bed," she said, even though it was only seven thirty.

"Night, sweetie," murmured her mom, buried in another pamphlet.

⁓

Hallie's side of the room had always been a chaotic mess. Every morning she slept until the last minute, threw on clothes from the floor, and dashed out the door with a granola bar. Now her bed had been meticulously made, her books lined up on the shelves instead of piled on her bedside table. Her clothes were all folded and back in her dresser, her shoes lined up in precise rows in the closet. Maren hated it.

A week after the accident, when it had become clear that Hallie wasn't coming home, her mother had gone on a six-hour cleaning spree. She'd dusted every corner of Hallie's side. She dragged the dust bunnies out from under the bed and then vacuumed and vacuumed and vacuumed the carpet. An hour later, Maren found her sitting on the floor, crying with the machine still running.

Every so often, Maren would rumple Hallie's blankets, toss her pillows around, pile up books on the bedside table, and lie there pretending her sister had only just gotten up for a glass of water. She made sure to tidy it all up again in the morning before her mother came in.

Now she sprawled on her own messy bed, pulled out her phone, and scrolled through her photos, going back in time. She lingered on her favorites. Hallie's grinning face beside hers with a rainbow arcing overhead. A lopsided cake with marshmallow eyes and an ice cream cone poking out of its forehead that was supposed to be a unicorn but looked more like an alien.

Maren kept scrolling, traveling back in time to when she and Amos were still friends. The photos made her stomach ache: The two of them at a baseball game in the city, pointing at each other with giant foam fingers. Amos with Henri perched on his shoulder with a wet parrot dropping sliding down the sleeve of his shirt (he'd chosen to take French at school and loved trading insults with the bird). Maren and Amos on Halloween, dressed up as zombie bananas, laughing so hard that Maren had cried off half her makeup.

She turned off her phone and plugged it into the charger. A tiny brown moth fluttered around the overhead light, so she switched it off and lay there staring at the glowing star stickers she and Hallie had arranged in their own versions of constellations. The Great Horned Owl, Snorticus the Warrior, The Two Sisters. She missed her old life so much, it felt like she was turning inside out. Soon Hallie would be at one of those facilities where people went when the hospital couldn't help them anymore. Where there was no hope of her going back to normal, of her coming home, of their family's life ever being the same again.

Maren prayed with every cell in her body for her dream cure to work.

Six

THE DREAM WAS ALWAYS THE same, a nearly perfect copy of the memory that flooded Maren's sleeping brain every single night.

She sat in the passenger seat of her dad's car, with Hallie at the wheel. Hallie had just gotten her license and their mom worried about her driving without a grown-up, but Maren needed a ride home from dance class and everyone else was busy. Maren had promised to keep an eye on her sister's speed and check for hazards and bad drivers along the way.

"And I know Ms. Marigold said no tights with runs in them, but it was just a tiny hole," said Maren, still upset about the stern talking-to she'd gotten after class. It wasn't her fault she'd tripped in the parking lot on her way inside.

"Hmm," said Hallie, flicking on her blinker.

"Are you even listening to me?" said Maren.

"Uh huh," murmured Hallie.

"You're *not* listening to me," said Maren.

Hallie sighed. "I'm concentrating on my driving."

"You can hear and drive at the same time." Maren picked at the hole in her tights, which had grown from the size of a pencil eraser to the size of a quarter. "What's going on with you lately?"

"Nothing." Hallie's voice was falsely bright.

"I don't believe you," said Maren. "You've been weird for a while now. Jumpy and secretive and stuff. I know you think nobody notices, but I do."

"Aren't you quite the little detective." Hallie's tone was unusually snide. Maren's fingernail snagged through her tights, making another hole beside the first one. She tried to ignore the sting of her sister's words and pressed on.

"Do you have a secret boyfriend or something?"

Hallie rolled up to a red light beside the marina where all the fishing boats docked. "No."

"A secret girlfriend?"

"No."

"Are you being tailed by the FBI because a kind, yet vaguely suspicious nuclear physicist asked you to hold on to her secret files and then disappeared?" Maren made a show of peering in the side mirror to see if anyone was following them.

"No." Hallie didn't laugh like she was supposed to, and a bolt of nerves shot through Maren. It wasn't like Hallie to keep secrets from her.

"What is it, then?" she whined.

"I told you, it's nothing." Hallie inched toward the red light. Their mother always waited at this intersection to make sure the other traffic had stopped before going through. She always repeated the same warning to Maren and Hallie: *Be careful here. People can't see the traffic lights well in the late afternoon sun. Always wait until it's safe to go.*

Maren was supposed to remind her sister of all these things. Her dream-self mouthed the words, but her voice made no sound.

The light turned green, and Hallie stepped on the gas.

A heavy old pickup truck appeared from nowhere. The air exploded and the car shot sideways and spun. Wheels screamed on pavement. Fragments of glass floated toward Maren, sparkling in the afternoon sun. Red flecks mixed with the glittering glass. Someone screamed, but Maren didn't know who. It might have been her. A black hole opened up in the place where Hallie sat. Maren couldn't see her. Couldn't look at that place. Couldn't look. Couldn't.

Her eyes flew open. Sweat drenched her sheets, and her pulse thundered in her aching head. Outside, rain drummed on the roof and gurgled down the gutters. She switched on her light to chase away the last traces of the nightmare, then buried her face in her hands.

Hallie, Hallie, Hallie.

Her beautiful, funny, absurdly smart sister. The one who'd taught her how to tie her shoes, how to read, how to sneak cookies from the kitchen without anyone noticing. Who had a black belt in tae kwon do and got the lead in all the plays. Who, even when they were arguing and hating each other, would battle to the death for Maren. Who walked all the way to Curtis Mayhew's house once just to tell him he was a lying, pus-filled pimple that deserved to be popped.

Maren hadn't reminded Hallie to wait at that traffic light, and now her sister was a doll in a bed. Maren didn't know if she was even in her body anymore—all the doctors' fancy words about brain function and prognoses didn't explain where Hallie really was, if the real *her* was ever coming back. But Maren couldn't let herself dwell on that; she just had to keep trying. She hoped with all her heart that Hallie was still in there, that she'd flown in her dreams today. And that the flying would start to heal her.

The little brown moth was back, hurling itself over and

over at Maren's light fixture, wanting something from the bulb that it couldn't give. Maren understood how the poor thing felt. She opened a wooden box filled with tiny dream sachets and took out a pure white one. It smelled like spearmint and cotton wool. An eraser dream. Nothing but clear white and softness. Eraser dreams left Maren feeling oddly empty the next day, but it was better than looping through the accident dream all night until she threw up. With a pang of guilt for erasing a dream of her sister, no matter how bad it was, Maren tucked the sachet under her tongue.

Seven

"RENIFLEUSE DE CHAUSSETTES SALES."

Ignoring Henri, Maren stepped around an antique butter churn and joined her grandmother at the counter. Lishta stirred something in a wooden bowl while Henri added small black objects, one at a time, with his beak.

"I still have no idea where he comes up with these things," muttered the old woman. "Your human-niece does *not* sniff dirty socks, Henri." She ruffled his gray chest feathers with her knuckle, and he let out a burbling chirp. "What a bird even knows about socks, I can't imagine. Watch out for that box of bee stingers, dear."

Even though the box of stingers was closed and sealed with duct tape, Maren gave it a wide berth as she stowed her backpack behind the counter. She peered into Lishta's bowl and instantly regretted her decision. Beetles floated in a lumpy, cheese-like substance.

"That's enough bugs now, Henri," said Lishta. The bird squawked and fluttered up to his food bowl, where he began flinging birdseed in all directions. "Maren, will you hold that cloth?" Lishta pointed to a second bowl, over which she'd draped a checkered square of fabric.

Leaning back as far as possible, Maren held the edges of the cloth while Lishta spooned the beetle-cheese mixture inside. Once it was all in, Maren helped her gather up the edges of the cloth and held them while Lishta tied a string around the bundle. The pungent liquid dripping out through the bottom made Maren's eyes water.

"I still don't get why anybody would buy this on purpose," she said, thinking of her car accident dream the night before.

Lishta carried the bundle to the fireplace in the corner and hung it from a hook in front of the smoking coals. Then she set the bowl under the bundle to catch the drips. "No matter how boring or sad people's lives are, they always seem better after a nightmare."

Maren wasn't sure she agreed. She missed her boring old life, and she wished getting it back were as easy as waking up. She missed the days when the worst thing that happened was having no clean socks because Hallie had stolen hers. Going back even further, she missed the days when she'd been able to walk through the halls of her school without jeers and whispers. The last year had tumbled downhill like a snowball on a mountain, building speed as it rolled. Picking up sticks and rocks and boulders. Crushing trees and people and buildings in its way.

Shuffle toe step shuffle toe step.

"Remember that woman who came into the store yesterday?" said Maren. Lishta nodded, and she continued. "I ran into her at the hospital afterward. In the children's ward."

"Oh?" Lishta opened a square glass jar and scattered white grains onto a sheet of paper. It was dreamsalt—dissolvable crystals that Lishta collected from some secret location she hadn't yet told Maren. Without one of these granules tucked in every sachet, the dreams wouldn't work. It also helped people to fall asleep and stay asleep for the duration of the dream.

"She was standing out in the hall, listening to us in Hallie's room," said Maren. "Ms. Malo, right?"

"Maybe Ms. Malo." Using tweezers, Lishta began adding dreamsalt, one grain at a time, to a row of half-finished sachets. "I'm not certain that's her real name."

"Why?"

"She wrote Sophia with a PH when she printed her name on the contract a few months ago, but then signed it Sofia with an F."

"That's pretty suspicious," said Maren.

Lishta blew gently on the dreamsalt to activate it. This was the part that nobody but the members of Maren's family could do—it was where their dream magic came in. "Many years ago, a girl around your age came into the shop, pale and shaking with rage. She wanted a nightmare—the worst nightmare in the entire shop."

Goose bumps whispered up Maren's arms. "What was her name?"

Lishta sighed. "I wish I could remember, dear. I asked her why she needed a nightmare, and she said it was for her brother. She said he'd slipped her something while she slept, and she'd dreamed she was being eaten by a python the size of a crocodile. It slowly swallowed her foot, her ankle, her knee—well, you get the idea—and she couldn't move or even scream."

Heel step heel heel went Maren's feet. She'd never heard of this particular nightmare, but it sounded hideous.

"The girl hadn't slept in weeks," said Lishta. "Every time she tried, the dream came back, even though she locked her bedroom door and window. You see, even after the nightmare was gone, its effects on her brain lingered." Lishta folded her knobby hands over her stomach. "This, my dear, is precisely why we have that rule about dreams and consent."

To hide her burning cheeks, Maren knocked a walnut off

the counter and crouched to pretend to look for it. She hadn't
given Hallie a nightmare, just a harmless flying dream.

"Of course, I couldn't sell that poor child a nightmare," said
Lishta. "I gave her an eraser dream free of charge, a handful of
calming dreams, a funny snake dream to counteract the effects
of the nightmare. I reminded her that we never sell nightmares
to minors, and I tried to persuade her that revenge wasn't the
way to heal. But she refused to listen. She called me a lot of bad
names and stormed out of the shop. I assume her family moved
away, because I never saw her again. Until a few months ago."

"I feel bad about what happened to her," said Maren.

"It was terribly unfortunate." Lishta wiped her hands on
her apron. "But I don't like that she's still looking for nightmares, and I especially don't like that she followed you. I'm
going to ask around, see if anyone remembers that girl and
knows her name. And if you see her again, please tell her I'd
like to speak with her."

The tightness in Maren's chest eased a little. At least one
adult agreed that something was weird.

"JOLIE JOLIE MADEMOISELLE!" squawked Henri,
pushing a brass safety pin along the counter with his beak.

"Did you ban her brother?" said Maren.

"I never met him," said Lishta. "I'd sold only one of those
python-swallowing dreams—to a middle-aged man, so I

assumed the girl's brother had stolen or bought it from him. I banned the man, just to be safe, and that's when I started locking up the nightmares."

Maren pictured a crocodile-sized snake with her leg halfway down its throat and shuddered. "I'm glad you did."

Lishta laid her wrinkly hand over Maren's smooth one. "Try not to worry about it, dear. Shall I tell you about that whispering dust I found?"

"Yes!" Maren shouted, startling Henri, who dropped his safety pin onto the floor and let out a long string of French swears.

Eyes twinkling, Lishta spun the combination lock of the safe. She pulled out the tin, slid open its lid, and shook a few flecks onto a white sheet of paper. Then she and Maren bent over it. It looked like ordinary dust, gray and dull. It smelled like ordinary dust, too, though Maren was careful not to sniff too hard and suck it up her nose.

"We've got at least twenty different kinds of dust already," said Maren. "What's so special about this?"

"There's a college right smack in the middle of Connecticut," said Lishta, wiggling a little with excitement. "Full of big old trees and red brick buildings. In the far-back corner of the center for the arts, there is a curving alcove under some stairs."

Maren waited, knowing that Lishta's stories usually didn't make sense until they were done.

"If you stand at one end of the curve with your head close to the ceiling and someone stands on the other side, you can whisper things, and they'll hear it like you're right next to them," said Lishta. "It's a whisper chamber. And I collected this dust from the inside of the arch."

"Sounds cool," said Maren. "What will it do in dreams?"

Lishta hopped from one slippered foot to the other in her own old-lady version of a tap dance. "It allows you to whisper through the layers of consciousness."

Maren cocked her head and stared at her dancing grandmother. "Layers of what?"

"Consciousness." Lishta nudged the edge of the paper and the dust particles shifted. "More plainly, it lets you talk to a dreamer as they're dreaming. They'll hear you inside their dream without waking."

Maren's imagination spun in a million directions, but the one it kept leaping back to was Hallie. She could ask Hallie to wake up. Give her a million reasons to get better, remind her of the life that was still waiting for her. Nine days was plenty of time to convince her.

"Can they talk back?" she said, nearly breathless.

"Maybe, maybe not," said Lishta. "People's words often

sound normal to them in their dreams, but they come out of their actual mouths as gibberish. Or there's no sound at all."

Maren's feet shuffled left and right. Even if Hallie couldn't respond, the fact that she might be able to speak to her was massive. Of course, there were a few minor obstacles. Number one was the fact that she shouldn't be giving Hallie dreams at all, let alone ones dosed with whispering dust. Number two was the fact that the dust in question was locked in a safe that Maren didn't have the code for.

"This is very dangerous stuff in the hands of the wrong person," said Lishta. "Imagine what you could do by influencing someone's subconscious. The things you could tell them, make them believe. Make them want to do."

Maren set her chin on the counter and waited for the dust to look different, do something, maybe whisper a little. "But what if it were the only way you *could* talk to someone?"

Lishta folded the paper in half and tipped the dust carefully back into the tin. "I know exactly what you're thinking, sweetheart, and the answer is no."

Tears pricked the corners of Maren's eyes. Lishta set her own chin on the counter beside hers and sighed. "I understand why you'd want to do it. It's very hard for me not to want the same. Everyone misses your sister like mad. But we don't know exactly how this stuff works, how much to use, what will happen. Her brain is still healing, and we wouldn't want to make it harder for her." Lishta caught sight of Maren's cringing face, and her voice softened. "Until we can test it out on a healthy person at least, it's just not safe, darling."

"PETITE SOURIS SOURNOISE." Henri zoomed down from the shelves, buzzed the top of Maren's head, and dropped a wrapped candy on the counter beside Lishta.

"Maren is not a sneaky little mouse." Lishta unwrapped the candy and popped it in her mouth. The harsh scent of clove stung Maren's nostrils. It was rude of Henri not to bring her one, too, but she was glad he hadn't. "Though perhaps it isn't a bad idea to test the dust on one," continued Lishta. She let out a thoughtful hum. "If only one of us could speak mouse language."

Maren rolled her eyes at the parrot, who busily scattered beetles across the counter. Lishta refused to put Henri in a cage—she said it gave him anxiety and terrible gas—and Maren always ended up cleaning up the stray feathers and droppings.

"You must promise never to tell anyone about this dust— or give it to your sister." Lishta's gray eyebrows formed a straight line. "The same consequences apply to you as everyone else. I'll have to ban you from the shop."

Maren's left foot slid out, tapped, then slid back in. "I

promise." Maybe if she kept this new promise, it'd lessen the wrongness of having broken the other one. Maren wondered if Lishta could see the guilt in her eyes.

An electronic melody trilled inside Maren's backpack. She dug her phone out, grateful for the interruption.

"Sweetie?" Her mom's voice, staticky and shrill. "Can you hear me? I'm at the hospital."

Maren's stomach plummeted. "Is Hallie all right?"

"Yes, yes," The line went crackly and then blank. Then Maren's mother's voice came back midsentence: "...not to read too much into it, but oh my goodness I just called your father and he—"

"Mom, wait." Maren cut in. "Can you start again?"

"She smiled!" her mother yelled. "And the nurse said she laughed for a couple of seconds."

Maren's phone slipped off her shoulder and almost fell. "Hallie did? When?"

Lishta lifted her eyebrows, and Maren gave her a giddy thumbs-up as her mother spoke.

"Very early this morning. I'm with her now, but she hasn't done it again. The doctors said it doesn't mean she's going to fully wake anytime soon, but it's a good sign."

I did that, thought Maren. *The dreams are helping her.*

"I'm coming there now," she said.

"That's great, sweetie. I really need to get to work now. I had to reschedule all my morning meetings for this afternoon."

"I'll be there as fast as I can." As she hung up the phone, Maren wanted to shriek with joy. "Hallie laughed!" she said to Lishta as she struggled into her backpack. The idea of having her sister back was Christmas and the Fourth of July and a litter of brand-new kittens and winning the lottery all rolled up into one stunning event.

"I'll bring the car around while you lock up." Lishta pulled her enormous, lumpy purse from a hook on the wall. She kissed Henri's feathered head and threw a handful of seeds into his bowl. "Look after the place while we're gone, Henri."

"AU REVOIR, PETITE CROTTE DE NEZ," said Henri.

Maren blew him a kiss and swung through the door into the typewriter shop, Lishta trailing close behind.

"Ahh!" A bearded, immaculately coiffed man leapt out of Maren's tornado path. It was Alexei Aliyev, one of the hairdressers from Mr. Alfredo's Splendid Salon.

"I'm sorry, we're just about to close," she said, her sneakers shuffle-dancing impatiently in the dust.

Alexei's mouth drooped into his beard.

"Hello, dear," said Lishta. "It's only for a few hours and then we'll be back. We've had a family...well, the opposite of an emergency. What do you suppose you'd call that? Antimergency?"

Alexei stuttered and mumbled and Maren just wanted to hurry him out of the store, but Lishta stopped to peer up at him. "Are you all right?"

"It's nothing." Alexei's beard trembled.

Lishta laid her hand on his forearm. "Tell me."

"For a week now, I've been having the most ghastly nightmare," he said. "I was hoping you could give me something to get rid of it?"

"There, there." Lishta said in a low and soothing voice. "Of course I can help. Why don't you tell me about this dream of yours?"

Shuffle ball change shuffle stamp. Maren wanted to feel sorry for Alexei, but she wanted to see her sister's wide-open blue eyes more than she wanted to feel sorry for him.

Lishta turned to her. "Sweetheart, why don't you hop on the bus? I'll meet you there in a little bit."

Ordinarily, taking the bus instead of riding with Lishta would have annoyed Maren. Today, she couldn't have cared less if she had to walk to the hospital. If she had to hop there on one foot. Barefoot.

"Hope you feel better soon!" Maren swung around Alexei, giving him a sympathetic but encouraging smile. "See you there, Gran-Gran."

Eight

THE BUS ARRIVED AT THE stop twenty seconds after Maren did. She bounded up the steps, paid her fare, and found a window seat all by itself. Luck sizzled in the air, making the edges of everything extra sharp.

Paradiddle paradiddle fah-lap heel heel toe heel went her shoes on the filthy floor.

The Green and Fresh was still closed, its entrance covered in swaths of yellow CAUTION tape. Men in white coveralls and netted hats stood out front, gesticulating wildly. They were probably figuring out a solution, like moving the wasps' nest somewhere else. Somewhere very far away, Maren hoped. She shuddered, brushed imaginary, deadly insects off her bare arms, and checked her backpack for the EpiPen. That wasn't enough to ruin her mood, though. She'd cured Hallie a full *nine days* early.

There was almost no traffic going down Main Street, because this day was full of lucky energy. As the bus zoomed past the harbor, a seagull swooped overhead, clutching a disco donut with flashing sprinkles in its feet. Maren laughed so loud that the couple in front of her turned around. She didn't care. The downhill-rolling snowball of her life had finally smashed into pieces, and inside was a gleaming nugget of gold.

At the hospital, Maren launched herself off the bus and dashed inside the building before it had time to pull away. The elevator doors opened before she even pressed the button, because today karma and fate were working together and they loved her. As she hummed upward, none of the usual elevator dread filled her stomach. Hallie was going to open her eyes again, and she'd see Maren and realize it was time to wake up permanently now.

Maren thundered down the hall of the children's wing. She stuck her tongue out at the smiling unicorn. Then she waved to the nurses at their station and was about to throw herself into Hallie's room when the door opened and an old man stepped out. It was Captain Perry, the man who'd accidentally hit them with his pickup truck. He had lived in Rockpool Bay even longer than Lishta. His fishing magic made sure that dolphins, whales, and sharks never got caught in his nets, and that only healthy, full-grown fish from sustainable populations did.

"Ahoy, Miss Partridge." Perry doffed his captain's hat and smiled sadly. He'd visited Hallie every day since the accident, reading books out loud and playing songs on his harmonica that all the nurses gathered around to listen to. Today he carried a leather-bound copy of *Treasure Island* and a travel magazine about Florida.

"How's she doing?" said Maren, itching to rush inside the room.

"Good, good," said Captain Perry. "I heard she let out a wee laugh earlier. What a sound that must've been! Let's hope she does it again soon."

"She will. I'm sure of it." Waving goodbye to Captain Perry, Maren slipped inside the room and shut the door.

Hallie's eyes were closed. The monitors beeped just like they always did. Her blanket lay folded straight across her chest.

"Hey, big sister." Maren loomed over her, watching carefully for the tiniest flutter of eyelash or lip, but there were no flutters. She blew on her sister's eyebrow. Still nothing. Maren pulled the chair up so close to the bed that there was no room for her legs, so she sat with them tucked up, elbows propped on Hallie's mattress.

And she watched.

And waited.

And watched.

"Gran-Gran told me more about that whispering dust," Maren said to fill the silence. "If you give it to someone while they're sleeping, you can talk to them inside their dream. Isn't that cool?" She sighed. "But she won't let me use any to talk to you. I have no idea if you can hear me right now. Can you?"

Hallie didn't answer. Rationally, Maren hadn't expected her to, but there'd been a dust-sized fleck of hope.

"Twitch your finger once for yes," said Maren, unwilling to let go of that speck of hope.

But Hallie didn't move. Not a twitch, not a blink, not a smile.

The clock ticked away the time, and Maren's foot tapped along. Her arms began to tingle. Her calves cramped. Her head grew heavy. She slumped back in her chair, still watching. The machines beeped and clicked, and Hallie didn't budge. Maren had to pee, but she feared she'd miss an important flicker of movement if she left.

"Wake up," she whispered. "Wake up wake up wake up."

A nurse wearing Mickey Mouse scrubs came in. "Hello, Maren," she said.

"Hi." Maren felt bad that she didn't know the nurse's name. "Has she laughed again yet?"

"Not since before your mom was here." The nurse adjusted Hallie's IV and wrote a few things on her clipboard. "I'm really going to miss her next week."

Maren gulped. "But she smiled, too?"

The nurse lowered her clipboard, and pity filled her eyes. "She did, and that's great progress. But Hallie's recovery is going to be a marathon, not a sprint."

Maren didn't understand why the nurse was handing her a tissue. Then she realized she was crying. She felt like a baby.

"Whittaker is better equipped for a marathon than we are." The nurse rubbed Maren's shoulder, which made her cry even more. Whittaker, like Sterling, was a long-term-care facility, not a place for people who had started waking up and returning to normal. It was even farther away than Sterling, almost an hour by car.

"Is there somebody we can call to come get you?" said the nurse, handing Maren another tissue.

"My grandmother is on her way." Maren's voice was thick with tears. Lishta should have been there ages ago, but apparently Alexei's problems were more important. "We thought Hallie was waking up."

"One day, I bet she will." The nurse's expression was one Maren recognized. It was the "Everything is fine, even though I have no idea if it actually is" smile she'd given Alexei earlier.

Maren snuffled into the tissues and muttered her thanks as the nurse left to check on other patients.

"Hallie," she whispered. "Wake up."

Maren's phone chirped. Reluctantly, she dragged her eyes away from her sister. Her screen filled with text messages from Lishta, who hadn't quite gotten the hang of cell phones.

My car wonton start

went start

My car will note startle

My car has broken I will bet here soon as i can

Maren stood and shook the pins and needles out of her legs. She checked to make sure Hallie was still breathing, then she looked for the tiniest hint of a smile on her lips, the smallest crease of a laugh line in the corners of her eyes. Nothing.

Maren's hand tiptoed to her pocket, where the two last flying dreams were nestled. She shot a quick glance at the doorway. Ten seconds later, the dream was tucked under Hallie's tongue. Maren stood beside her sister and waited as the clock ticked away the seconds. One minute. Two minutes. She checked Hallie's mouth and the sachet had dissolved, but not a muscle in her face had moved. Maren began to pace. Ten minutes. Twenty. When people dreamed, their eyes twitched and darted around beneath their closed lids, but Hallie's weren't doing that. The dream should have started ages ago, but her face remained listless, her lips almost white.

It wasn't working.

Maren ran out into the hall. She ran all the way to the double doors, slammed through, and kept running. Her feet didn't want to stop to wait for the elevator, so she found the stairwell and clattered down.

Be careful on the stairs, said her mother's voice in her head, and she wanted to be careful because the last thing her mother needed was two daughters with head injuries, but she just couldn't stop. Finally she hit the ground floor with both feet, barged through the lobby, and threw herself outside.

Across the parking lot, the bus pulled away from the stop. Maren slumped against the scratchy brick side of the building. There was no luck in today after all. Nothing had changed. She'd given her sister a silly dream that made her laugh but not wake up. Dreams weren't medicine. She drooped down to sitting on the gum-encrusted pavement.

A pair of high-heeled shoes appeared beside her. A withered, brown rose petal floated down and landed on Maren's knee.

"Excuse me," she said, brushing the petal off.

"No, I don't think I will." A woman's voice, sharp as a spike.

Maren looked up so fast she almost tumbled over sideways. "You again."

The woman from the dream shop—Maybe Ms. Malo— shrugged and peeled another petal from a bouquet of crusty, dead roses. Perched over her left ear was an orange moth with black circles that looked like eyes on its wings.

"I saw what you gave your sister," she said, gazing out across the parking lot. Her false eyelashes were thick as paint- brushes. Maren tried to stand, but the woman had dug the heel of her shoe into the hem of her long T-shirt, pinning it to the ground.

"So what?" Maren folded her arms and tried to look like she was perfectly happy where she sat.

"You're not allowed to give dreams to non-consenting people," said Maybe Ms. Malo.

"It's not allowed for *you.*" Maren fought to keep her voice even. "Those of us who work at the shop don't have to follow that rule."

Another petal landed in Maren's hair, and she swiped it off.

"I think you're lying," said the woman.

"It's a free country." Maren let out a tiny cough. "You can think whatever you want."

The pointy toe of the shoe swung sideways, but the heel remained sunk into Maren's hem. Underneath the shoes, the woman wore pale pink tights. "I wonder what your dear grand-mother would say if she found out what you'd done."

"She wouldn't care." Maren hated how nervously shrill her voice sounded.

"Let's find out, shall we?" The women pulled a sleek silver phone from her bag. "I've got her phone number right here."

Under normal circumstances, Lishta would never believe a random stranger's story about Maren. But only a few hours ago, Maren had specifically asked about giving Hallie dreams. Her head began to spin.

The woman's nails tapped at the screen of her phone, and Maren heard the other end ring. If Lishta believed the truth, she'd ban Maren from the shop. Maren couldn't bear the thought of losing all the knowledge she'd gained, all the wisdom of collecting and measuring and mixing. Even more than that, Maren loved spending time with Lishta.

"Hang up!" she squeaked. The woman lifted a meticu-lously plucked brow, and Maren added, "Please."

From the phone came Lishta's muffled voice: "Hello? Hello? Is someone there?"

Maren made frantic cutting gestures at the woman. If Lishta banned her from the store, she'd have to go back to rattling around her empty house all day while her parents worked and Hallie was a vegetable miles and miles away. She'd have no friends, no sister, no parents...and no grandmother.

"Please," she said again, and this time her voice broke.

The woman's thumb hovered over the screen.

"Just tell me what you want," said Maren.

Maybe Ms. Malo's plum-colored mouth flattened like a snake's as she slid the phone back into her bag. "I want a dozen nightmares," she said, and the ice in her voice made Maren shiver. "I want the worst dreams you've ever made. Those last three didn't quite cut it."

Maren gulped hard. "We have all kinds of nightmares. If you just come to the shop tomorrow, I can—"

"Do I look like an idiot?" The woman ground her heel into Maren's T-shirt, tearing a hole through to the pavement. "You'll bring me those dreams tomorrow, and you won't breathe a word to *Gran-Gran* or I'll tell her you've been messing with your poor sister's brain."

Maren wanted to shove the woman, kick her in the shin, push her into a dumpster. But she was trapped, and the woman knew it. "Why do you want so many?" she said. "You can just buy them three at a time. Nobody needs more than three nightmares a night."

Maybe Ms. Malo scoffed. "I've got a rather...hearty appetite for them."

Maren couldn't imagine the effects of taking so many nightmares at once. That kind of terror could really change a person. Maybe it already had. Maybe they weren't all for her. Maren's skin went clammy.

The hospital doors whooshed open, and a boy in a blue soccer jersey came out.

"Amos!" Maren shouted, waving both arms and wishing she could stand up.

Amos looked startled by her sudden outburst of friendliness, but he veered toward them. The pointy-toed shoe lifted from the edge of Maren's T-shirt, and she sagged with relief.

"Tomorrow. Here. Same time." The woman dropped her bouquet of dead roses and stalked off.

Nine

"Who was that?" Amos picked up the withered remains of the rose bouquet from the pavement.

"A customer." All of a sudden, the parking lot pitched and tipped and swirled with watercolor smears. Maren laid her head on her knees and prayed she wouldn't throw up in front of Amos.

"She's creepy," he said, cramming the dead flowers into a nearby trash can.

"I know." Slowly, the nausea eased as the click-clack of the woman's heels faded. Maren looked up just in time to see her climb into a green sedan.

"What was she saying to you?" said Amos. "It looked like she was standing on your shirt."

"She, uh, just wanted to talk to me about some stuff from the store."

"Typewriters or dreams?"

"Does it matter?" Even though she felt bad about his grandfather, Maren didn't want to talk to Amos any longer than necessary. He'd become friends with the one person who made Maren's life a living nightmare, and when she had told Amos he had to choose between her and Curtis, Amos had chosen the bully.

"Hey, is that her again?" Amos pointed to a green car that had circled the perimeter of the parking lot and now rolled toward them. Maren caught her breath as the car drifted past and Maybe Ms. Malo held her gaze. There was something unfathomable in the woman's dark eyes, something cold and reptilian.

"Do you think we should go inside until she's gone?" said Amos.

Taillights flashed as the green car rounded the corner. Maren shuddered and nodded. Maybe hanging out with Amos wasn't the worst option.

He let her go through the doors first. "Should we tell somebody about her?"

"No!" Maren didn't mean to yell, but did. The last thing she wanted was that creepy woman telling the hospital staff she'd been slipping things into coma patients' mouths.

"*Ooookay*." Amos flopped in a chair in the atrium and pulled out his phone.

"Don't give me that look," said Maren.

He tapped at his screen. "What look?"

"The one that means I'm weird and you're normal and I'm somehow endangering your health with my weirdness."

Though he didn't look up from his phone, the corner of Amos's mouth twitched.

"And if you're texting Curtis about me, I swear I'll punch you," said Maren.

Amos's laughter echoed through the high-ceilinged space. "I'm texting my mom. She wants to know what time I'm coming home."

"Oh." Maren couldn't remember the last time her mom had asked her that question. They spent so much time at the hospital that it was pointless. Sometimes it felt like she'd lost her parents in this accident, like she'd gone invisible to them in their new lives that revolved around work and the hospital. Only Lishta noticed her anymore.

Maren wondered what would happen if she called the police. Maybe they'd arrest the woman for harassing and blackmailing a child. But if they pressed charges, there'd be a court case and the woman would get a chance to speak, and she'd tell everyone what Maren had done. Maren couldn't let that happen.

"You hungry?" said Amos.

Maren's stomach rumbled. "A little." This was an understatement. She hadn't eaten since breakfast.

"They have really good cake in the cafeteria," said Amos.

"The *hospital* cafeteria?" Maren had eaten enough gray hamburgers and crunchy pasta in the days following the accident to be very suspicious of Amos's statement.

"Yeah." Amos hopped out of his chair and tripped over his shoelace. "I know it's gross in there, but you have to trust me on the cake."

Maren glanced out at the parking lot. No sign of Lishta yet—or Maybe Ms. Malo's green car. Her stomach gurgled again. She took out her phone, but there were no new messages from her grandmother, so she wrote her own.

I'll be in the cafeteria.

———

Amos was one hundred percent right about the cafeteria cake. Maren had a hard time not shoving her face straight into the monstrous slice of dense chocolate spackled together with whipped cream and cherries. She wasn't sure if it appeased her hunger or her guilt more, but either way, she felt better.

"Did you hear about Maisie Mae's?" said Amos, who was working on his second slice of cloudlike coconut cake. His hair was longer than it used to be, curling around his ears and corkscrewing over his forehead.

"No, what happened?"

"All the ice cream melted last night. The freezer seems to be working fine, and nobody can figure out what happened." Amos shoveled a hunk of cake into his mouth and continued talking around it. "They're going to have to close for like a week while they make everything from scratch all over again."

First the grocery store, then the ice cream shop. And Hallie wasn't waking up. Maren wondered how she'd ever thought Rockpool Bay was full of luck today.

"How's your sister?" asked Amos.

Maren's chocolate cake turned to paste in her throat. "They said she smiled and laughed for a second, so I rushed here." She set down her fork and blinked hard at the table so Amos wouldn't see the tears. "I really thought she was waking up. But I've been staring at her face for like three hours now, and she hasn't moved an inch, and I feel like I just can't be patient anymore. I want to scream."

"That's a good sign that she did all that stuff, though, right?" said Amos.

"It is." Maren stabbed her fork into a lump of frosting. "But they're going to transfer her to this faraway long-term-care facility in nine days. It really hurts to keep hoping."

Amos chewed for a long time, then took a gulp of his milk. "This is my grandpa's third heart attack. Every time it happens, I keep thinking this is it; he's going to die, but then he doesn't. The thing is, he's forgetting more stuff every time it happens." Amos's eyes flicked to Maren's and they were a little watery, too. "It's sort of like the opposite of hope."

"I'm sorry," said Maren.

Amos mashed his cake into a flat pancake. "I just wish I wasn't the only one visiting him all the time. I'm scared he's going to die while I'm here and I won't know what to do."

"One time I was visiting Hallie while my parents were at work," said Maren. "All of a sudden, her machines started beeping and the nurses rushed in and they called the doctors and made me go out in the hall. All I could think was that Hallie was going to die and my parents weren't going to be there with her. And it somehow felt like my fault."

They were both quiet for a while as Amos molded his cake into something resembling a fortress and Maren tapped through her recital routine under the table.

"Who did you get for homeroom?" he said finally.

"I didn't look at the list," said Maren. "I want to transfer somewhere else, but my mom won't let me, so I'm ignoring September as long as I can."

Amos ripped open a packet of sugar and sprinkled it

around the edges of his fortress so that it looked like sand. "I told Curtis to stop saying all that stuff about you."

"Well, he didn't," said Maren. "And it didn't stop you from hanging out with him."

Amos became very absorbed in raking the sugar sand with his fork. Maren slid her plate away. "Why are you friends with that kid? He's probably not even nice to his dog."

Amos shrugged guiltily. "His parents got divorced last year, and his dad moved out of state, too. We don't talk about it much, but sometimes I feel like he's the only person who really gets what it's like."

"Maybe I don't get what it's like, but I tried to be there for you, too," said Maren.

"I know." Amos sunk low in his chair. "But you had this, like, *perfect* family, and it was hard to be around sometimes."

Maren probably wouldn't have agreed that her family was perfect at the time, but she'd give anything to have it all back, to have the privilege of fighting with Hallie over bathrooms and socks.

"Curtis isn't that bad when other people aren't around," said Amos. "That time in the playoffs when I couldn't stop the last kick in the penalty shoot-out and we lost, he invited me over his house for pizza. I guess I thought I'd convince him to be nicer and we could all be friends. But then you flipped out and blocked my number and wouldn't answer the door or my emails, and I was all alone and didn't know what to do." Amos set down his fork. "I tried, too, you know."

Maren thought of all the crummy, spiteful names Curtis had called her. She hated the way other kids laughed along, just because it meant he wasn't making fun of them. She abhorred his mean little tactic of repeating the same fake stories over and over until they stuck and people started believing them. He'd made up so many lies about her over the years that she'd lost track of them all, but a few lingered painfully:

Maren ate a bunch of nightmares when she was a baby. That's why she's such a freak now.

Maren's so gross, she has to put secret ingredients in those dreams she sells to make people like her.

Maren's sister has a different dad. That's why she's so pretty and Maren looks like a troll.

Maren shoved her chair back, and the screech on the tile echoed through the room. "Just because he's nice to you, that doesn't erase the fact that he's horrible person," she said. "Thanks for the cake."

"Wait," called Amos, but Maren didn't look back.

Ten

"THERE YOU ARE!"

Maren jolted awake. She'd been curled up like a cat in the chair beside Hallie's bed. Lishta's apron hung askew, and one of her braids had come unpinned. It pointed off the side of her head like an antenna.

"You said you'd be in the cafeteria," she said, sitting on the edge of Hallie's bed and picking up one of her limp hands.

"I was in the cafeteria for a long time," said Maren. "And then I left."

Lishta crinkled her already crinkly forehead. "What's wrong?"

Maren was about to say *nothing*, but she swallowed the word. "I guess I was the only one who thought Hallie waking up was a big enough deal to spend the whole day here. But I guess I was also the only one silly enough to think she was actually going to wake up."

"Oh, love." Lishta pulled Maren out of her chair and folded her into the softest hug Maren had felt in a long time. "I'm sorry, I'm sorry. My car battery died, and I had to ask Alfredo to jump-start it for me. Then when I finally got on my way, the back bumper fell off."

Her car was an original Volkswagen Beetle from the 1960s. Maren was honestly surprised the bumper hadn't fallen off before. It probably had.

"Then the car behind me ran over it." Lishta's eyes narrowed. "Of course, if he hadn't been tailgating, he would have had plenty of time to stop. We had to wait for the police, and then I had to duct-tape my bumper back on until I can get it properly repaired."

"That stinks," said Maren, though she felt that her day had been worse.

"Your mother will be here soon," said Lishta. "Do you want to wait for her, or shall I bring you home?"

"I just want to go home," said Maren. She felt guilty about leaving Hallie, but she just couldn't hope any more today. And she needed to figure out how to get the nightmares for that woman.

Lishta nodded, and her eyes were soft. "Of course."

Maren followed her out into the dimming evening and was relieved to see no trace of the creepy woman or her car. Lishta's yellow Beetle sat near the entrance. Silver tape covered the entire back of the vehicle, all the way up to the rear window, though Lishta had left the license plate and taillights exposed. It was hard to tell where the bumper even was.

Lishta proudly inspected her handiwork. "That thing won't be falling off again anytime soon."

Even through her misery, Maren was spellbound. "How many rolls did you use?"

Lishta silently counted on her fingers. "Sixteen. It was lucky the hardware store was still open."

Maren squeaked open the passenger-side door, yanked on the front seat until it pitched forward, and crawled into the back. Over the years, Lishta had repaired the seat with almost as much duct tape as the bumper. As the familiar smell of gasoline and lemons and tape enveloped her, Maren closed her eyes and inhaled deeply.

"Did you see that woman again today?" Lishta asked.

"No." Maren's foot gave a guilty little shuffle step.

"Good," said Lishta. "She didn't come to the shop, either, though I haven't had any luck in finding out her name. Let's just hope that's the end of that."

Maren rubbed her thumb along a crease of silver tape.

She wasn't sure she believed that Maybe Ms. Malo was only taking the dreams herself, considering she'd tried to give her brother a nightmare as a child. But the consequences of not obeying her were too severe. Hopefully once Maren handed over the dreams, that would be the end of it. But she'd have to steal them when Lishta wasn't at the shop, because she wasn't allowed to touch the nightmares unsupervised. They were too dangerous if they started to leak.

"Look," said Lishta, slowing and pointing to a pink building. A tall, spindly man pushed a paint roller up and down its front wall, slowly turning it black. "Didn't you have a party there once?"

Maren peered through her dusty window. "That's the Zottery family's paint-your-own-pottery shop."

"Used to be," said Lishta, pointing to the rainbow-colored Zottery Pottery sign, which lay on top of a pile of trash by the street. A new sign had been propped up against the building's door. In swirling silver letters on a black background, it read, "Coming Soon: The Nightshade Emporium."

"Is the pottery shop moving?" Lishta waved to the man, who had turned to peer at them. His stringy, braided goatee reached midway down his chest, and he'd gathered what little hair he had left into a thin ponytail, with a round patch of bald on top of his head. He didn't return her wave.

Maren pulled out her phone and typed in the name of the store. A rainbow-colored website covered in paintbrushes flashed onto her screen, with a banner across the top.

"After many beautiful decades in Rockpool Bay, our family is moving to New Zealand. Zottery Pottery's last day of business will be Saturday, June 10. We'd like to thank all of our customers for their wonderful artistic contributions over the years, and we wish you all the best!"

Maren's stomach sank. Tara Zottery was a year behind her in school. Her family had clay magic; they sculpted the most intricate, whimsical creations and let people paint and keep them for a small fee. Maren hadn't been there in a few years, but the shop's presence had been comforting, full of happy memories from her childhood. Now another part of her old life—and Rockpool Bay—was disappearing.

The spindly man set down his paint roller and stalked toward the car. "Can I help you with something?" His voice was low and slithery, and it sounded like the last thing he wanted to do was help. If a centipede could talk, Maren thought, it would sound exactly like that.

"I don't like the look of that guy," she whispered.

"Neither do I." Lishta gave the man a little salute and stepped on the gas. Once the pottery shop had disappeared around a bend, she sighed.

"I'm sorry you got your hopes up so high about Hallie. I suspect the next few weeks will be full of those ups and downs. If you don't want to come into the shop, I understand."

"No, I do," said Maren. "It helps to keep my mind busy, actually."

Lishta flashed her a smile in the rearview mirror. "And I love having you."

The pool of warmth in Maren's stomach lasted about three seconds before freezing to ice as she remembered what she had to do. She had to steal a dozen nightmares by tomorrow afternoon. Lishta usually arrived at the shop just after dawn to get started on mixing, so it would be hard, if not impossible, to get there before her. Even if she managed, it would look incredibly suspicious, considering Maren never went to the shop before ten.

She'd have to do it tonight.

Maren's pulse rocketed as Lishta turned onto her maple-lined street. Tonight she would go back to the shop and steal the nightmares. It would be scary to go there alone, and very wrong, but then it would be over. Maren couldn't even look in Lishta's general direction as the car pulled up to her little ranch-style house. All of its lights were off.

"Shall I come in and make you some dinner?" said Lishta.

"No, it's fine." Maren opened her bag and pretended to

look for her keys so she didn't have to make eye contact. "I'll heat up some frozen mac and cheese. It's really good," she added, wincing at the lie that Lishta would surely recognize.

"All right, sweetheart. Good night."

Lishta didn't back out of the driveway until Maren had closed the front door and turned on the living room light. As the car's headlights faded, she slumped against the wall. Her stomach whined with hunger and nerves—the cake hadn't been enough food, but she worried she'd throw up if she ate anything else.

Pulling out her phone, Maren checked the bus schedule. The last one home came at eleven o'clock. That gave her two and a half hours to steal the nightmares. There was just the problem of her parents coming home and finding her gone. Maren tapped out a text message to her mother:

I'm home. Where are you?

A few seconds later, her mother's response popped up.

Hospital. Gran-Gran told me she brought you home. Did you eat?

Yeah. What time will you be home?

About an hour.

I have a headache and am going to bed.

OK sweetie, sleep well.

Trying not to let her mother's lack of concern bother her, Maren went to her room. She lined up some pillows on her bed and pulled her flowery comforter over them. It looked nothing like a sleeping person, and she wondered how anyone pulled it off in movies. With a frustrated huff, she rifled through her bedside table drawer and pulled out a flashlight, which she tucked into the pocket of a black hoodie. The clock read eight thirty-five. She'd miss the bus if she didn't hurry.

Maren stared at the pillows on her bed, willing them to look more person-like, but it was useless. She opened her window a few inches so she could get back inside later on. Then she clicked the lock button on her doorknob, let herself out into the hall, and closed the locked door behind her.

In the kitchen, Maren pulled out her mother's grocery notepad and pen. Under a list that said only "Salt," she wrote:

> I'm in bed. Please don't disturb me. I already
> took a Tylenol.
> Love,
> M

Her parents wouldn't leave her alone in her room forever, but it might buy a few hours. Especially if they were tired and preoccupied with Hallie stuff. Leaving the kitchen and living room lights on, Maren slipped out the front door, into the shadows and cricket song.

Eleven

THE STREETLIGHTS CAST ROUND PUDDLES of yellow on the sidewalk as Maren jogged toward the bus stop. Though her neighborhood lay miles from the ocean, the air was damp and salty and faintly blue-tinged. Heavy clouds of fog came whispering in, blurring the stars and the edges of everything.

Most of the people on Maren's street were home for the evening, the multicolor glow of television screens flashing in their windows. Maren wondered how many families were sitting together, arguing over what show to watch. Not realizing what a fragile thing they had. She'd give everything she owned to be able to sit on the couch again with Hallie, wrestling for the remote.

The lights in Amos's old house were out, and on a whim Maren stole into the backyard, pulled a nail file from her bag, and scraped a few splinters from the side of the deck. She plucked three leaves from a forsythia bush, scooped a pinch of dirt from the old sandbox, and tucked everything inside the spare plastic bag she kept beside the EpiPen in her backpack. She still hadn't decided about making that dream for old Mr. O'Grady, but it didn't hurt to have the ingredients.

On the main road just outside the neighborhood sat the empty bus stop. The air had grown darker and colder and foggier, and Maren wanted to run back to her house, but that wasn't an option. She zipped her sweatshirt up to her chin and perched on the edge of the bench. With every car that flashed past, wiry curls of fear twisted through her chest.

This is the same bus stop you go to every morning, she told herself. *It's exactly the same place as before, just dark now.*

A dirty white delivery truck rumbled by. The driver turned to look at Maren, his face a blur of shadows, and she shivered and pulled up her hood.

Shuffle step shuffle step shuffle ball change.

She wondered if Maybe Ms. Malo knew where she lived. Peering into the shadowy bushes, she listened for rustling or creeping sounds, but all was silent except for the crickets. Maren wanted to crawl under a blanket on her couch, turn on her dancing show, and forget about everything. But tomorrow would come no matter how she ignored it, and that woman would be waiting.

The bluish fog thickened, and night slithered around the lonely bus stop. Finally, two halos of headlights appeared, along with a groaning engine roar. The bus driver said nothing as Maren fed her quarters into the slot. The only two other passengers were a college-aged girl and a man who had fallen asleep with his head against the window. Maren chose the seat behind the girl and pulled out her book, though she just stared at the same line of meaningless words as the bus clanked and roared and stopped and started into town.

Even the waterfront felt weird tonight, its dazzling lights a muted green haze in the fog. The air no longer smelled of cinnamon; salt and copper and something dank and mossy tickled Maren's nose. A chattering tourist family boarded the bus, and the woman gave her a long look. Maren suspected she had that motherly instinct of knowing when someone else's child was up to no good. Quickly, she turned away to look out the window. The harbor was nearly invisible. Tiny waves lapped at the shore, raucous laughter carried down from the pier, and Maren wondered how organ music could sound so merry in the sunshine, yet so sinister in the dark.

The bus groaned up Main Street, and the street grew quieter as they left the restaurants and shops behind. Maren pushed the button for her stop. By the time the doors opened in front of the dark post office, the sidewalks were completely empty.

She leapt out before anybody could ask where she was going or where her parents were. As the bus pulled away, she locked eyes with the tourist mother through the window. The wires of fear in Maren's chest twisted deeper, and she dashed away down the dark cobblestones. Her foot stomped into a puddle, splashing cold water up her leg, but she barely flinched. There could be muggers and murderers lurking out here. Or that woman from the hospital. Maren wished she'd brought a weapon. One of her mother's cooking knives or a can of mace, though she didn't know anybody who actually owned one.

A single streetlamp in front of the typewriter store cast the building in eerie blue shadows. Maren slowed as she crept closer, peering carefully at the trash cans in the alley. Even the cement planters full of flowers loomed ominously. She leapt over their reaching shadows, and with trembling fingers she pulled the shop key from her pocket.

A gust as warm as someone's breath tickled the back of Maren's neck, and she bit back a scream. But no one was there. With her heart bashing her ribs, Maren unlocked the door and threw herself inside the shop.

"Prrp?" came Artax's cat voice from across the dark room.

"It's me." Maren left the lights off so nobody would see her from outside. Artax bumped against her shin, and she scooped him up, cradling him like a baby against her chest as she threaded her way through the typewriters. He wouldn't be much protection against whatever might be lurking in the dark, but his soft fur and quiet purring made Maren feel a little safer.

As she turned the doorknob leading to the dream shop, a sledgehammer of guilt hit her. She was stealing from her own grandmother. Lishta had always given Maren any dreams she wanted and probably would have given her the nightmares if she'd asked. But she couldn't ask.

A night-light plugged into the far wall cast the dream shop in a faint, spooky glow. It smelled vaguely of cheese, and the butter churn still sat in the middle of the floor. Even though Maren knew this shop as well as her own house, everything felt different tonight. She couldn't shake the thought that the dreams were creeping out of their boxes and jars, floating through the dark, ready to slip inside her mouth or her ear. Maren crept around the butter churn, pressing her nose to the top of Artax's head.

"I see you," came a whisper.

Maren stumbled backward and nearly dropped the cat.

"I sssseeeee you," the voice rasped out again, coming from

the top of the shelves. It took Maren several tries to make her voice work.

"H-Henri?"

A whirring of feathers, and the bird landed on the counter. Henri cocked his head and gazed at her with one beady, emotionless eye.

"When did you learn English?" she stammered.

"HOMARD POISSEUX," he said.

Still shaking, Maren pushed the rolling ladder over to the nightmare cabinet. It was hard to say which dreams were the worst in the shop, since different things were scary to different people. A bathtub full of spiders would be horrifying to most people but probably just inconvenient, or maybe even fascinating, to an arachnologist. Fires were a common fear, as were plane crashes. But Maren needed something utterly terrifying if she wanted to satisfy this woman. She was far too scary herself to be fazed by a standard bad dream.

Maren turned on her flashlight, found the key for the nightmare cabinet in the drawer where Lishta had hidden it, and climbed the ladder. At the top, she dried her sweaty hands carefully, leaned around the ladder's side, and unlocked the cabinet. She couldn't see the box of nightmares that she had in mind, but it had to be there somewhere. People rarely asked for this kind of dream. Maren slid canisters and jars out of the way, trying not to think about the nightmares sneaking out.

Then she spotted it: a small slate box with a dust-coated lid, all the way at the back. Maren nudged it with her flashlight until she could reach, and as her fingers closed around its sides, the faint scent of decay wafted out. Holding her breath, Maren climbed down the ladder and set the box and her flashlight on the counter. Artax hissed and went back through the doorway to the safe typewriters. Even Henri hopped away from the box, murmuring something in French.

Maren found a plastic bag, turned it inside out on her right hand, and lifted the box's lid with her left. The sachets inside were jet black, and they emitted the faintest smell of what could only be described as fear: oily and metallic with an underlying hint of rot.

Lishta had made this batch of nightmares about a year ago, before Maren was allowed to help. She'd scraped splinters from the inside of a coffin and ground up the leg bone of a deer she found dead on the side of the road. Maren had asked what the dream was about, but Lishta had been reluctant to tell her everything. Very loosely, she said, it was about being locked in a coffin and buried alive. And not being the only thing in the coffin. And the other thing in the coffin was whispering your name.

Maren shuddered as her plastic-bag-covered fingers closed around the sachets, and quickly she turned the bag inside out and zipped it shut. She wondered why Maybe Ms. Malo would choose to sink into such deep horror.

Something darted at the flashlight beam, and Maren leapt away. It flapped and circled—a pale blue moth as long as her finger. Maren grabbed a tissue and flapped it at the moth, and it blundered away to a window where faint light filtered through. As the insect skittered against the glass pane, Maren tried to slow her breath.

She checked the time: nine thirty. Her mother would be home any minute. Maren slid the lid back on the slate box and shut the cabinet. Just before she climbed down the ladder, she stopped and stuck the key back into the lock. Pulling out random boxes without looking at their labels, she added several more sachets to her plastic bag. Just in case.

"Voleuse, voleussse," hissed Henri. Maren had never heard him whisper before. Now that she had, she preferred the screeching. She tucked the plastic bag of nightmares into her pocket.

"You'd better not tell Gran-Gran I was here," she said. The joke sounded weaker than she meant it to. She wondered if Henri really could tell Lishta. The bird squawked and flapped up to his perch on the ladder.

Maren let out a sigh of relief as the shop door closed behind her, shutting away all those nightmares that might have been swirling around in the dark. She wiped her hands on her jeans, in case any dregs had gotten on them.

"Bye, Artax." She felt reluctant to let her only friend go, but she couldn't dither in the shop.

Outside, beyond the small patch of lamplight, everything was shadow and fog, and the salty wind kept slithering in from the sea. Maren could barely make out the alley leading back to Main Street. Hunching her shoulders, she stuck her hands in her pockets, then remembered the right pocket held night-mares. Her shiver became a shudder.

As she tiptoed through the alley, water plinked behind her. On second thought, maybe it wasn't water; maybe it was footsteps. The click-clacking of someone wearing high-heeled shoes. Someone trying not to make noise. Maren stopped. The tapping stopped. Gulping down the rock of fear lodged in her throat, Maren started walking again.

Click clack click clack.

Closer now. Something small and flitting grazed the top of Maren's head.

She broke into a run.

Out on Main Street, in a swirling bank of blue fog, a figure sat hunched on the bus stop bench. Maren slid to a halt a few yards away, gasping as much from fear as from running. The figure turned to peer at her through the gloom. It was the spindly man from the pottery shop, now wrapped in a black coat. He held a pipe in his long fingers, and as Maren approached, he exhaled a plume of smoke that swirled into the shape of a bat and flapped away into the starless sky.

"Why are you out so late, little girl?" The man's centipede voice raised goose bumps on Maren's arms. He tapped the embers out of his pipe onto the pavement and stowed it away in his pocket.

She shook her head, not trusting her own voice and also following the rule about not talking to strangers. Especially strangers in empty places at night. Places she had no business being alone. Places where nobody would hear her scream. Maren eased her phone out of her bag, tipped the screen away from the man's flinty gaze, dialed the numbers nine, one, one, and let her thumb hover over the "send" button. If the bus didn't come in a minute or two, she'd walk down toward the waterfront and pick it up at another stop. But from out in the cloudy blue darkness came the click-clack of those shoes.

Maren took a few more steps away from the man and stood with her phone at the ready. If she could just manage to stay safe, to not panic, and to get on the bus, this would all be over soon.

Click clack click clack.

Maren gritted her teeth so hard they made a crunching sound. She couldn't keep her eye on the dark alley and the man at the same time. He let out a wet, phlegmy cough and took a small box from his pocket. Humming quietly, he unfolded its waxed-paper lining, pulled out a clump of stuck-together lozenges, and popped it into his mouth. Then he held the box out in Maren's direction and gave it a shake.

"These'll clear out that frog you've got stuck in your throat," he said.

It wasn't a frog; it was a rock. Maren licked her papery lips and checked that the numbers were still on her phone screen. No bus. She never should have come out here alone. She should have waited until tomorrow and figured out a way to distract Lishta so she could steal the nightmares in broad, safe daylight. She could have made Lishta extra cups of tea and gotten the nightmares when she went to the bathroom. Maren was furious with herself for not thinking of that. If she got herself kidnapped, it would devastate her parents. They'd been through enough already.

The man shook his box of cough drops again, and the smell of his breath wafted over: sour cherry menthol mixed with sardines and smoke. Maren's eyes began to water. It wasn't crying—only babies cried when they were scared.

"No, thank you." Her voice flew out firm and angry.

"So you *can* speak." The man twisted his braided beard and smirked. "Suit yourself. I got the last box before they shut down."

Maren glanced across the street at the pharmacy and realized its windows were boarded up. A black sign like the one outside Zottery Pottery sat propped beside the door. COMING SOON: THE MONKEY'S PAW, it said, and underneath the silver script was a grisly illustration of a disembodied monkey's hand, its dried-up fingers curled into a claw.

"Are you taking over the pharmacy, too?" said Maren.

The man's thorny laugh made her stomach clench. "I'm a business associate of the new owner," he said. "But it's not going to be a pharmacy anymore."

Maren looked at the black and silver sign and tugged her sweatshirt zipper up tighter. Someone had once tried to sell Lishta a monkey's paw like that, but she'd refused, saying some items were too disgusting even for nightmares.

"Things are changing here," said the man, and Maren hated that she had to agree. The pharmacy had been in business for fifty years and carried a few charmed remedies for things like toothaches and gout. This made four businesses in a week that were either temporarily closed or out of business. Something was rotten in Rockpool Bay. And Maren suspected she knew who this man's business associate was.

Finally, *finally*, headlights flashed and an engine rumbled, and Maren almost cried with relief as the bus drew nearer, a glowing beacon of light and stars and normalcy. She stood with her toes hanging off the edge of the curb as it slowed, and she jumped through the doors before they were fully open.

"You getting on?" called the driver to the spindly man.

The man winked at Maren and shook his head. Nerves crawled like invisible spiders over her skin. She chose the seat right behind the driver, took out her book, and didn't look up until she arrived at her neighborhood stop.

Maren had never, ever been so happy to see her house. The television glowed in her living room window now, too. Anybody passing by would have thought they were just another normal family. Maren could almost pretend it, too, as she crept around the side of the house.

She got a metal bucket from the toolshed and stood on it to pry open her window. There was no graceful way to climb through the narrow frame, so she slid, headfirst, and landed, headfirst, on the braided rug.

She was back. She was safe. The dark, foggy town was miles away, and so was the spindly man and the Monkey's Paw and whatever had been click-clacking around the alley. Maren locked her window, ripped off her sweatshirt, and shoved it under the bed. From out in the living room came the sound of televised laughter and cheering. After changing into her pajamas, Maren padded down the hall, wearing the exhausted expression of someone who'd been battling a headache. She hoped she didn't smell like salty night air or bus fumes or guilt.

But she needn't have worried. Her parents were fast asleep on the couch, her dad with his feet on the coffee table and her mom with her head on his shoulder. They looked so worn and vulnerable—smaller than usual, somehow. Maren gave them each a kiss on the forehead and went to the kitchen to make herself a sandwich.

Twelve

"Five, six, seven, eight!"

Ms. Marigold's voice rang through the dance studio, and seventeen dancers launched into the opening steps of their routine. In the second row, second from the left, Maren shuffle-ball-changed and hopped, sweat dripping down the back of her leotard. She flung her arms wide, kicked, and spun, hitting a perfect double pirouette and launching into the next sixteen-count tap sequence.

For the first time in days, she felt good. She felt *incredible*. Dancing meant she had no brain space to think about comas or nightmares or who might be getting those nightmares. Her brain held only the music, the counts, the steps, and the clack and slap of her shoes on the floor.

"Excellent!" crowed Ms. Marigold as the dancers hit their final poses and the music ended. "Again!"

With a breathless laugh, Maren ran back to her starting position, set her hand on her hip, and waited for the song to begin. The dancers had reached that giddy end-of-class state where they knew the routine well enough to fling themselves through it, putting their own personal spin on the steps and fully letting go. It was the closest thing to a flying dream, Maren thought, as her shoes skimmed across the floor and the music filled her whole body. She never wanted it to end, never wanted to stop moving, never wanted to go back to real life ever again.

But after three more repetitions of the wonderful, zooming routine, dance class ended.

"Fabulous job, everyone!" said Ms. Marigold as the dancers ran for their towels and water bottles. "Maren, you were on fire today. What's gotten into you?"

Metric tons of guilt and a desperate need to escape reality. Maren smiled and shrugged at her teacher. She wished she could stay for the next class, but it was ballet, and Maren was decidedly not a ballerina. Plus her parents couldn't afford any more classes. She felt bad enough taking this one, but her mom had said that dance class would be the absolute last thing on their list to cut. After groceries and heating, she'd said, and even though Maren knew that was a joke, she loved that her mother knew how important it was to her.

"See you all next week," said Ms. Marigold as the dancers filed out of the studio. Maren lingered in the changing room, not ready to face Maybe Ms. Malo. But it needed to be done. The euphoria that had fizzled through her veins all through dance class slowly drained away as she guzzled the rest of the water in her bottle. She shoved her tap shoes into her backpack, where a packet of nightmares lay nestled, and headed outside.

As Maren approached the hospital's automatic doors, they swished open and Maybe Ms. Malo glided outside. She wore sunglasses and a leopard-print dress that hung off her stick-straight frame. A scarlet moth with a body like a feather duster perched on her belt. Without a word, she walked around the side of the building. Maren hated the assumption that she'd just follow like a dog, but she did. The woman leaned against the brick wall and held out her hand, palm up.

Maren hung back as close to the hospital's entrance as she could. "You can only have these if you swear you're not giving them to anybody else. And you have to promise you'll leave me and my family alone after this."

The woman let out a wolfish laugh and pulled out her phone. "Come here, darling. I've got something to show you."

"I'll wait here, thanks." Maren crossed one ankle over the other and folded her arms. She still had some leverage while she held onto the dreams.

"I don't think you'll want anyone else seeing this." The woman held up her phone. Its screen showed a video of a hospital room. Maren squinted. That was Hallie's hospital room, and Maren sat beside her sister on-screen. Her legs went numb.

Maybe Ms. Malo paused the video and beckoned to Maren again, and this time she moved closer, floating like a balloon tied to the woman's wrist. That couldn't have been what she thought she saw. It wasn't possible.

But it was. The video had been shot from somewhere to the left of Hallie's bed. Judging from the picture's fuzzy edges and the long stalk of green running up the side, the camera had been hidden in a flower arrangement. Maren watched herself glance nervously at the door and then begin to sing happy birthday to her sister.

"No," she whispered, wishing she could scream through the camera, through space and time and warn her past-self not to do what she was about to do. But past-Maren slipped out of her chair, still singing, and leaned over Hallie. The camera zoomed in. Past-Maren glanced straight at it, unseeing, and then opened her sister's mouth. She took a tiny something from her pocket and placed it in Hallie's mouth. The worry and hope etched all over her past-self's face cut Maren deep, made her want to sob with frustration and fury.

"How dare you?" she said as the video cut out.

The woman slid her phone into her purse. "I hope you've brought me truly horrific nightmares."

Maren nearly choked on her rage. "These dreams are so frightening, my grandmother won't sell them to most people."

Maybe Ms. Malo smirked. "If you're lying, I'll send this video straight to your grandmother *and* all of your sister's doctors. And post it on the internet for good measure."

Maren gaped. She couldn't think of a single thing to say.

"I'm sure you know it's against hospital rules to feed magical things to poor, unsuspecting coma patients." The woman's voice was ice and razor blades. "I'm also sure Rockpool Bay has laws about using magic on people against their will. You won't be allowed to set foot in this building again. Or in Sterling or Whittaker, whichever your parents end up choosing."

Hot acid swam up Maren's throat. She pulled the plastic-wrapped nightmares from her bag. "Take them," she said. "I hope they scare you to death."

Just you and nobody else. Maren's whole body thrummed with guilt. Giving away nightmares was the worst thing she'd ever done, and she hated herself for being so selfish. But it wasn't just about her. It was about healing Hallie, too, and their family. The last thing Maren's parents needed was a scandal on top of everything else.

The tall woman unwrapped the dreams, sniffed a black sachet, then gave a little nod. "I'll need another dozen tomorrow."

"Another *dozen?*" Maren only had six nightmares left.

"And I'd like some of that whispering dust."

Maren's knees almost buckled. She wondered how the woman knew about the dust, then realized with a shudder that there must be more than one video of her and Hallie. This also meant, without a doubt, that the evil woman was giving the nightmares to other people. Otherwise, there'd be no need for the whispering dust. Maren felt like a worm. Worse than a worm. A slug.

"I can't give you whispering dust," she said. "Even *I'm* not allowed to touch it."

"I don't care how you get it," said Maybe Ms. Malo. "Make it happen."

"But that's not fair," said Maren. "We had a deal."

The woman's eyebrows stretched into an exaggerated

display of pity. "Did you really think so? That's sweet, but no. You're mine now, Maren Eloise Partridge."

Black stars spun in Maren's vision. She was going to be sick.

"You'll bring the dreams and the dust," said the woman, "or everyone will know what you did."

Maren spun on her heel and ran. Ugly, shrill laughter chased her around the corner of the hospital, past the entrance and into the parking lot, where the bus pulled up to the stop.

"Wait!" Maren's desperate shriek rang out.

The doors opened, and Amos appeared on the steps, about to exit.

"Hey." His grin faded to concern as he took in Maren's flapping clothes and ragged expression. "What's going on? Is she back?"

"No." Maren wanted to get around him, but he blocked her way. "I just need to go home." She wedged her elbow between him and the door and tried to squeeze past.

Amos didn't budge. "Is your sister okay?"

"She's fine!" spat Maren. "Can you please just move? You're holding everybody up."

"She's right," said the bus driver. "Keep moving, kid."

Amos gave Maren a long look that said *I see you*. Then he stepped aside. Maren tripped up the stairs and dropped one of her quarters. It rolled down the aisle and she chased after it, crouching and cursing. By the time she finally found it under someone's grocery bag, her breath came in gasps and tears dripped off the end of her nose.

As the bus pulled away from the hospital, Maren realized she'd forgotten to visit Hallie.

Thirteen

DUMPING HER BAG AND SHOES on the floor, Maren climbed
into bed with her clothes on. Her whole body ached with
exhaustion and regret. She'd played right into the trap, and she
couldn't begin to think what that woman was doing with those
nightmares. But she couldn't imagine never being allowed to
visit her sister again, and she couldn't stand the thought of
getting banned from the dream shop. She'd be stuck all alone
while her parents worked, drifting around like a sad little ghost.

Even though it was only midafternoon, Maren opened
the wooden box on her bedside table and pulled out a sachet
in the palest shade of robin's egg blue. She'd made this dream
when Lishta had first started teaching her to craft memory
dreams. It was clumsily made, a beginner's effort, but it didn't
matter. Maren had made a Hallie dream, crafted from a strand

of her hair, a clipping of grass from their backyard, and threads from their mother's old beach blanket. She tucked the sachet under her tongue, lay back on her pillow, and closed her eyes.

—

She sat, braiding her sister's long blond hair, on a striped blanket in the middle of a wide, green lawn. Everything beyond the grass blurred, but it didn't matter because the only thing Maren cared about was Hallie, whose back felt warm and solid against her knuckles as she braided. The air smelled of sunshine and freshly mown grass; birds chattered and chirped. Maren gathered and twisted, twisted and gathered, and the braid grew and grew until she had to coil it up in her lap. Still more hair remained to braid, but Maren didn't mind. She loved her sister, loved sitting here with her under this dazzling sky.

The deep green lawn began to ripple and curl. It formed big, rolling waves, taking Maren and Hallie's blanket with it. Up and down they drifted, up and down. Maren pulled an elastic from her wrist and tied off the end of Hallie's braid. Up and down, up and down. She gathered the length of braid that had been coiled in her lap and wrapped it around Hallie's waist and hers. Then she leaned her cheek against Hallie's back.

"We're safe as long as we're together," she whispered.

Hallie didn't turn around, but Maren knew she was listening. The braid would keep them safe, no matter what.

⁓

Maren woke to a rich, oniony cooking smell. She pulled the blanket over her head, shut her eyes, and tried to fade back to Hallie, to that sun-bathed dream, but only fragments remained. The softness of Hallie's shirt under her cheek, which was also the softness of Maren's pillow. The lingering, ghostlike presence of her sister.

"Come back," she whispered, but it kept fading. Maren had to be careful not to gorge herself on these dreams, because reality hurt a thousand times worse after they wore off. She kicked away the blankets and lay there, letting the fragments float in the edges of her mind. As she inhaled more of whatever was cooking in the kitchen, her stomach began to gurgle. She heard her mother's voice, then her father's. Maren glanced at her clock. It was only six thirty. They never *both* got home this early. She wondered if something was wrong, if they'd somehow found out what she'd done.

With a bat flapping around in her stomach, Maren tiptoed down the hall, straining to hear what her parents were saying. Then her mother burst out laughing, quickly joined by her father's low guffaw. Maren couldn't remember the last time they'd laughed like that. She dashed into the kitchen and found both of her parents leaning against the counter, a pot of soup simmering on the stove.

"Oh good, you're awake," Maren's mom cranked the pepper grinder over the steaming soup.

"What were you laughing at?" Maren leaned against the opposite counter, afraid to break this fragile and rare moment of happiness.

"There's a new sandwich guy at the lunch place next to my work," said Maren's dad. "And they have this special where you can get half a sandwich and a cup of soup. So the lady in front of me orders the special and asks for half a turkey sandwich."

Maren's mother's shoulders shook as she stirred the soup. She knew what was coming next.

"So the guy makes a turkey sandwich, cuts it in two, and gives her half. And then he leans over the counter and says to me"—Maren's dad's voice dropped to a whisper—"I never know what to do with the other half."

Her mom let out a blare of a laugh, a sound Maren hadn't heard in ages. Her dad waited for her to do the same.

"I…don't get it," she said.

"He could just cut one piece of bread in half to make the half sandwich." Maren's mom took a sip from her glass of wine.

Her dad picked up a knife and started slicing bread. He'd even stopped at the nice bakery to get a French baguette.

"Oh, right." Maren felt silly for not thinking of that, but her parents were happy and this was so rare and she should try to be happy, too. Even though…

Maren pushed the idea out of her head. Even though nothing.

"I bet he has a whole stash of half sandwiches somewhere," said Maren's mom. "He probably smuggles them out when he leaves at night."

Maren's dad grabbed a slice of baguette, stuck it down the front of his shirt, and sauntered out of the kitchen, whistling. Her mom laughed so hard she had to set down her glass, and when he came back and mimed shoving more bread in his pockets, Maren couldn't help but join in the laughter. It felt like they were a different family tonight, like they were figuring out a new way of being fun with only the three of them. If only Hallie were here to see it.

Maren's laughter died in her throat, though the tears in her eyes stayed. She pulled a paper towel from the roll above the sink and dabbed at her face.

"How's your head today?" said her mom.

"Better, I guess."

Maren's mother laid the inside of her wrist against her

forehead. She complained about always having cold hands, but they felt wonderful on Maren's head when she was sick. Maren wished the chill could seep through her skull and soothe the chaos in her brain. She knew she should tell her parents what was going on with Maybe Ms. Malo. Everything had gotten so snarled up, she had no idea how to untangle it.

"No fever," said her mom. "But I think chicken soup is still in order."

"You made that for me?" Maren was so used to everything revolving around Hallie that this one pot of soup felt extravagant.

"Well, it's not *all* for you." Maren's dad handed her a bundle of spoons and napkins. She rolled her eyes and set the table. Then she sat with her parents and quietly ate her soup while they chatted.

"I had an idea for a new dream today," said Maren's mom.

Maren almost choked on a noodle. She couldn't remember the last time her mom had talked about dreams. "What is it?"

"You know those dreams where people show up at school or work naked?" said Maren's mom. Maren and her dad nodded. "I was thinking it'd be nice to make something that counteracts them. Instead of suffering from naked shame, you'd arrive in class or at your office wearing the most stylish, beautiful, *comfortable* outfit with lots of pockets, and everyone would compliment your impeccable taste and ask where you'd gotten it."

"I love that," said Maren, who had suffered from the dreaded naked school dream a lot recently.

"I'm thinking ink and cotton," Maren's mother closed her eyes. "Licorice root for confidence. And the corner of a fashion magazine cover. Not cotton, actually. Cashmere."

As her mom listed ingredients and weighed the pros and cons of using natural versus synthetic fibers, Maren lined up the words in her head.

Remember that woman I thought was following me? Her name might be Ms. Malo, and she really is following me.

But then she'd have to speak the rest of the words.

I gave Hallie dreams after you told me not to. I stole nightmares from the shop and gave them to that woman. I'm pretty sure she gave them to unsuspecting people around town. I broke all of our family's most precious rules.

In this exact moment in time, her parents were happy—it was so wonderful to hear her mom talk about things that weren't coma or money related, and Maren knew that spilling the truth would be horrible and shocking and ugly. It would wreck this one perfect evening that they all so desperately needed.

Everyone finished eating, and Maren still hadn't worked

up the courage to let the words out. She washed the dishes while her dad dried.

"Want to put on the dancing show?" Her mom sat on the couch, holding out the remote.

Maren picked up Hallie's favorite throw pillow and tucked it into the corner of the couch. Then she scrolled through the shows and found the next episode. Her mother was already buried in another brochure.

Imani went first. She wore a yellow dress that made her look like a bird, and her music fluttered and soared, too. As Maren's favorite dancer slid through a quadruple-pirouette-back-walkover combination, the phone rang.

"Hi, Ma," said Maren's mom. "No, it's fine. What's up?"

Lishta's voice sounded shrill, though Maren couldn't make out the actual words.

"Another one?" said Maren's mom. "This is getting really weird."

Maren paused her show. Her mom mouthed the word *sorry* at her, then stood and gestured for her to continue watching the show. "Hang on a second, Ma. I'm going in the other room."

Part of Maren wanted to follow her mother and ask what happened. Another part of her already knew. *I'm doing this for Hallie and for them,* she told herself, but that wasn't exactly true. Mostly it was for herself. With guilt pinching her insides like tiny crabs, Maren settled uneasily back on the couch and unpaused her show.

Fourteen

"It seems you've gotten out of bed on the wrong foot today, sweetheart," said Lishta.

Maren was supposed to be pouring a jar of muddy tide-pool water through a strainer, but she'd managed to splash it all over the counter three times in less than five minutes.

"VOLEUSE!" yelled Henri.

"Stop that," said Lishta. "Your human-niece isn't a thief."

Maren glared at the bird as she mopped up the dirty water once again. Brown stains covered her T-shirt, and her thumb oozed blood from where she'd stabbed it while sewing up sachets.

"Is something wrong?" Lishta took a saltine cracker from the plate she was sharing with Henri and munched on it while staring thoughtfully at Maren. "Aside from the usual, of course."

Maren wanted to spill everything like she'd just done with

the tide-pool water. Maybe if she confessed, Lishta would only ban her from the shop for a few months. She could handle that. But if Maybe Ms. Malo showed the doctors her video, there was no telling how long she'd be banned from seeing Hallie. Possibly forever.

The door swung open, and Edna Frye barged in, wearing her post office uniform. "Lishta," she boomed, thumping her sturdy elbows onto the counter. "I've got a problem, and I need your help."

"Let me guess," said Lishta, who had turned a little pale. "Nightmares?"

"All week." Edna mopped her forehead with her polyester sleeve and dragged her fingers through her poodle-permed hair. "Same dream every single night. And this morning I found a note on my kitchen table saying if I wanted them to stop, I'd better leave town."

Maren hissed in her breath. Carefully, she screwed the lid onto the tide-pool water.

"Do you have the note?" asked Lishta, and Edna took a folded sheet of paper from her back pocket.

Lishta's fingers trembled as she pulled on her glasses. "It appears to have been typed on a very old machine."

"You've got a few of those," said Edna, jabbing her thumb in the direction of the typewriter showroom.

Lishta's mouth opened, then closed. She cleared her throat. "Tell me about the nightmare."

"I was out on a fishing boat—looked kind of like Captain Perry's," said Edna. "And then this giant whale showed up. Bigger than the whole post office, I swear. All covered in stripes, just like a tiger. Its mouth gaped open, all watery and sloshing and full of teeth." She swallowed, looking a little nauseous. "I kept trying to steer the boat away from it, but I couldn't. Then the steering wheel fell off in my hands and, well, you can guess the rest." Edna rubbed her bleary eyes. "I'm not scared of whales in real life, but that monster was something else."

Lishta sighed. "It's one of our dreams."

But it wasn't one of the nightmares Maren had stolen. The store hadn't carried that dream for months. Her racing heartbeat slowed from ninety miles an hour to eighty-seven.

"I'm terribly sorry this is happening to you," said Lishta.

Edna grimaced. "I don't want your sympathy. I want to know what's going on here."

Lishta pulled a hairpin from her braid and tapped her nose with it. "Have you made any enemies recently?"

Edna gave her a blank stare. "No."

On wobbling legs, Maren climbed halfway up the ladder to put the jar of tide-pool water away.

"No arguments with anyone in your household?" said

Lishta. "Or with someone who might have access to your bedroom when you're asleep?"

The postmistress folded her arms across her broad chest. "I live alone, and everyone in this town likes me."

Maren thought of all the times Edna had snapped at her for not standing in the right line at the post office. That seemed unlikely.

"Well, that settles it." Lishta poked the hairpin back into her braid. "We've got a nightmare thief on our hands."

The jar of tide-pool water slid out of Maren's fingers and teetered on the edge of the shelf. As she lunged to catch it, her foot slipped off the ladder and she swung sideways, nearly taking out an entire row of dreams and ingredients.

"MALADROITE," yelled Henri.

"Careful, dear," murmured Lishta.

It was true. They did have a nightmare thief on their hands. She was teetering on a ladder, about to explode into a million tiny, glimmering particles of guilt.

"We'll get to the bottom of this, Edna," said Lishta, opening jars and boxes and stuffing sachets into a plastic packet. "In the meantime, here's what I want you to do. Do you have any knee-high stockings?"

Edna lifted an eyebrow.

"Yes, I know it sounds rather bizarre," said Lishta. "But

if you can cover your mouth while you're sleeping, but still be able to breathe, it'll make things harder for anyone trying to slip you nightmares." She pondered a box of light-yellow sunshine dreams, then added three to the packet. "I recommend those knee-high nylon stockings you can get at the drugstore. Whichever color you like. Put it on your head and roll it down over your face before you go to sleep."

"You can't be serious," sputtered Edna.

Lishta leaned across the counter and squeezed her hand. "I am. Until we know what we're dealing with, it's better to be safe than sorry."

"You need to keep a better eye on those dreams," said Edna. "People shouldn't be able to just give them out like that."

"You're absolutely right," said Lishta. "I'm going to lock the rest of our nightmares in my safe and stop selling them until we find the culprit. In the meantime, please take these, free of charge." She held out the packet she'd put together. "It's an assortment of our most carefree and comforting dreams. And the white ones are erasers, just in case you do somehow end up with a nightmare again."

Edna's nostrils flared. "I'd rather not mess with any more dream magic."

"I understand." Lishta pushed the packet closer. "But please take them, just in case you change your mind."

"You'd better get this figured out fast," said Edna. "I'd hate to have to go to the police. You and I both know how flustered they get with magical affairs."

Lishta nodded, her face grim. "I assure you I'll do everything in my power to get to the bottom of this. And I appreciate you coming to me first, Edna. Take care, and remember the knee-high stockings."

Muttering about not having time for this kind of nonsense, Edna left the shop with her dreams. Lishta let out a shaky breath and bit into a saltine. Maren wondered if it were possible for a person to burst into flames from guilt. She had to come clean—this entire situation had gotten out of hand.

"Gran-Gran?" she began.

"Yes, darling?" Lishta said.

"There's something I have to tell you." Maren's nerves sputtered like a car running out of gas.

Lishta set down her saltine and peered at Maren. "What is it?"

"I… There's this… I mean…" Maren gulped and tried to figure out how to explain that she'd broken the rule but it wasn't her fault. The words refused to come out. "Do you think Edna will be all right?" she finally said, hating herself for being so spineless.

"Of course she will." Lishta's smile didn't quite reach her

eyes. "That woman is tougher than nails. Tougher than iron rail spikes, I'd say. It'd take a lot more than a few nightmares to run her out of town."

But the Zottery family had left town. Maybe somebody had been threatening them, too. Even though they'd moved away before Maren started stealing nightmares, it probably wasn't a coincidence. Hot shame washed over Maren's face.

"I almost forgot to tell you," said Lishta. "I found out that little girl's name. The one who wanted revenge on her brother." She pulled a slip of paper from her apron pocket and slid it across the counter.

Obscura Gray, it said in Lishta's old-fashioned cursive writing. Maren shivered. It felt like just thinking the woman's name might summon her.

"I met an old neighbor of hers, and then I looked her up on the *internet*." Lishta's proud tone made it sound like she'd traveled to the moon to get this information. "She moved away from Rockpool Bay as a teenager and became a ballerina, a principal dancer with the Copenhagen Ballet Theater. Quite a remarkable achievement, I'd say."

"Did she retire or something?" said Maren.

"The articles were rather vague, but it seems she left the company about a year ago," said Lishta. "There was no mention of why, and nothing's been written about her since. She seems to have disappeared. Until she showed up at our shop, that is. I've put out a few feelers around town to see if anyone else has spotted her, and your mother said she'd help me do some more internet searching."

Maren reached for the slip of paper. "Can I have this?"

"Of course."

She tucked the paper in her pocket. This was exactly the information she needed. Proof that Maybe Ms. Malo wasn't a maybe after all. She was a real person with a real name. With a reputation and international fame. Who could be traced by the police and arrested. Not that Maren was planning to go to the police. This was just leverage. She would threaten to expose Obscura if she didn't stop demanding nightmares, and the evil woman would have to give up.

Maren stoppered a vial of milkweed fluff and stuck it inside the drawer of an old card catalogue. "Do you need me to do anything else?"

"I don't think so." Tucking her apron up, Lishta stepped onto the ladder. Henri fluttered to her shoulder and began whistling a sea shanty as she climbed. "I'm going to take inventory of the nightmares before I put them in the safe."

Maren's thieving fingers went tingly as Lishta pulled out a slate box—one of the containers she had stolen from the previous night—and lifted its lid.

"Then I'm heading over to the hospital," continued Lishta. "Would you like a ride?"

Maren threw her backpack over her shoulder. "No! I mean, no thanks. I have some other stuff to do later, so I need to go now."

The whistling paused—"VOLEUSE!"—and began again.

"Goodbye, dear," called Lishta as Maren escaped the shop.

Fifteen

Obscura Gray stood waiting in the usual spot beside the hospital. The deep purple moth on her handbag matched the shade of her lips, which curled into a greedy smile as Maren hurried toward her.

"Did you give nightmares to Edna Frye?" said Maren. "And tell her to leave town?"

The tall woman shrugged. "Perhaps."

"Perhaps?" said Maren, unfolding the sheet of paper from the dream shop and holding it up. "Perhaps I should go to the police and the Rockpool Bay News and tell them you're illegally using magic and blackmailing an underage kid, *Obscura Gray.*"

Obscura let out a shrill laugh and knocked the paper out of Maren's hand. "You think knowing my name changes anything? Go ahead and try calling the newspaper and the police. I'll disappear faster than you can blink—I've done it before." She stretched out a sharp-tipped black shoe and flexed and pointed her foot. "And don't forget I can still send anonymous emails and videos while I'm missing."

Maren wiped chilly sweat off her upper lip. "When will this be over?"

"Once the nightmares have served their purpose." Obscura's flat tone raised goose bumps on Maren's skin. There were so many dreadful possibilities in that single sentence.

"I can't give you any more." Maren opened her empty hands at her sides.

Obscura's painted face twisted with rage, and Maren's skin tingled with the same foreboding sensation she got when a thunderstorm came rolling in across the bay. The tall woman steadied herself, smoothed down the front of her impeccably tailored suit, and bent her lips into a smile. "Why not?"

"My grandmother locked them in the safe with the whispering dust, and I don't have the combination." Maren prayed Obscura couldn't smell the nightmares nestled in the bottom of her backpack.

Obscura tutted and sighed. "Well then, I'm afraid this is the end. I hope you enjoyed your time with your sister…

and at dear old Gran-Gran's shop. It's about time for her to retire anyway."

"What are you talking about?" said Maren.

"All evidence of those rogue nightmares points straight to your grandmother." Malice gleamed in Obscura's dark eyes. "She did create them, after all. I dare say if you call the police, they'll figure it all out pretty quickly, including the typewriter she used to write those incriminating notes."

Maren thought of the mountain of old typewriters waiting to be repaired in the stockroom. There was no way of knowing if Obscura had used one of them. "But that's absurd," she said. "Why would anybody believe she was sneaking around giving people nightmares? And then trying to get them to leave town?"

"There are many reasons why a person might want to rid a town of all the other magical people." Obscura tapped her narrow chin thoughtfully. "As for the regular people…"

"What regular people?" said Maren, but Obscura ignored her.

"Doesn't she sell some kind of calming dreams for them to take after they have a nightmare? Seems like a good way to keep them coming into the shop and spending money. And then there's the footage of you slipping dreams into the mouths of unconscious hospital patients."

"My own sister!" Maren fought the urge to stomp on Obscura's pointy shoe. Again, the woman continued like she hadn't spoken.

"If all of that gets out, I don't think anybody's going to want to buy your dreams anymore…or even your typewriters." Obscura's purple lips turned down in an exaggerated pout. "Assuming the police let you keep the shop open, which seems unlikely."

Maren swallowed hard. Losing the shop would be horrible. Losing the respect of everyone in Rockpool Bay would be even worse. Those customers had trusted Maren's family, and she had betrayed them by helping this awful woman mess with their innermost thoughts and feelings. Maren deserved their hatred, but the rest of her family would be ruined, too. They'd have to leave town.

"I'll…I'll need to make the nightmares myself," said Maren. "It'll take a couple of days." Her dreams wouldn't be as scary as Lishta's or Hallie's, but that wasn't a bad thing. That should be the goal, in fact. Something like the pyramid-teddy-bear dream, but less obvious. Less silly. "And I still probably can't get the whispering dust."

Obscura shook her head. "You have one day. I don't care what you need to do, but you'd better figure it out."

Maren hated her disdainful tone, like she was used to

ordering people around and had never been questioned or challenged in her life. Maren wasn't anybody's servant. She took a couple of steps toward the front of the hospital, then stopped.

"Are you still afraid of snakes?" she said.

Obscura's eyes bulged. She stuck her hands behind her back, but before she did, Maren saw they were clenched into white-knuckled fists, and she knew she'd found something. A tiny hole in a stocking that might turn into a giant, ripping run if she pulled on it. She just wasn't sure how yet.

"You have one day," growled Obscura.

"I'll do my best," said Maren, and she ran to the front doors and let them swallow her up into the hospital.

Hallie lay slightly crooked in her bed. Maren wished it were because she'd moved, but the nurses had probably reconnected her tubes or given her a sponge bath. Hallie would die of humiliation if she knew people were giving her sponge baths. She didn't look humiliated, though. She looked asleep and a little deflated, like always. Maren shut the door tight, checked the room and all the flower arrangements for hidden cameras, and pulled the chair up close to Hallie's bed.

"A world-famous ballerina is blackmailing me," she

whispered. "Isn't that ridiculous? But it isn't actually funny. She saw me giving you dreams, and now she's forcing me to make nightmares for her. I can't tell anybody, because if I do, Gran-Gran's shop will have to close and she might get arrested and I won't be allowed to visit you anymore."

Maren imagined her words slipping down her sister's ear canal, reaching her brain and penetrating through the coma fog. She was torn between hoping Hallie could hear her and hoping she couldn't, because it was all so sad and unfair and Hallie had enough problems as it was.

"I don't know what to do," she whispered. "I know what I *should* do, but I don't think I can. I just wanted to fix everything so you wouldn't have to go to that long-term facility, but I'm making it all worse."

Shoes squeaked out in the hall, and Maren held her breath until they passed. She got up and checked the door one more time, then pulled a robin's-egg-blue sachet from her pocket. It didn't matter if Obscura was filming—she already had more than enough to ruin Maren.

"I made this," she said as she tucked it under her sister's tongue. "It's not very good, but it's based on a memory of me and you. Just in case I can't come visit you for a while and you can't remember why you need to come back. Please come back. Preferably within the next seven days, okay? I love you, big sis."

Maren watched Hallie's unmoving face for a long while and then she tiptoed out of the room, careful not to disturb her sister in case she was dreaming.

———

As the elevator doors opened to the lobby, Maren spotted Amos sprawled in a chair. He put away his phone and let out an exaggerated yawn, stretching his arms wide.

"I'm starting to think you're following me," said Maren.

"I swear I'm not," said Amos. "I was on my way home, but then I decided to hang around and make sure that lady wasn't here being creepy again."

You're about an hour late for that, thought Maren. But the fact that he knew something was wrong, even though he had no idea what exactly, made her feel a little less alone.

"She's gone." Maren felt more hopeful than certain about this. "How's your grandpa doing?"

"His heart is better, but his memory isn't." Amos shrugged in a casual way, but his eyes were a little watery. "We're moving him into a nursing home next week."

Another long-term place where nobody was expected to get better. Maren's heart hurt for Amos and his family.

"What are you doing now?" she said.

Amos looked startled. "Uh, probably going home?"

"Do you want to come with me to the pier? I have to collect some ingredients for dreams."

"Sure." Amos didn't hesitate for a second, and Maren's shoulders eased a little. "Can I help?"

"Okay," said Maren.

Sixteen

"SINGING BUBBLES, FIVE DOLLARS A bottle!" called the freckled woman. A couple wearing identical Rockpool Bay T-shirts
stopped to inspect her wares while their three kids raced in
circles, singing along with the purple bubbles and trying
to clap them between their hands. The late-afternoon sun
glinted off the harbor's flat water and gulls wheeled overhead.
Chattering tourists jammed the pier, looking for dinner and
entertainment and maybe a little bit of magic.

"You hungry?" Amos inclined his head toward the disco
donut machine, which blared thumping music from the
seventies. No one knew who operated the machine or how it
worked, but the donuts that came out were covered in flashing
sprinkles and were utterly delicious.

"Not really," said Maren, thinking of Obscura, of Lishta and Hallie. "Go ahead and grab something if you want."

While Amos waited in line for a donut, Maren wandered down the row of fortune-tellers' brightly colored tents. In the midst of the striped yellow and red and blue cabanas, she discovered a new one, midnight blue with silver moons and stars stenciled across the top. While all the other tents flapped gaily in the breeze, this one stood silent and still.

A man came barreling out from between two cabanas. His braided goatee swung over his dark T-shirt, and Maren gasped. She flattened herself against the midnight-colored tent as he barged past, not bothering to excuse himself. As the spindly man rounded a corner and disappeared, Maren sagged with relief. He didn't seem to have recognized her.

The wall of the tent rippled against Maren's back, and she leapt away as the entrance flap swung open. A woman wearing a long, velvet dress emerged, haloed in a cloud of acrid-smelling smoke. Her moon-white hair hung down past her waist.

"Would you like a reading?" The woman's bright yellow eyes fixed on Maren, making her feel dizzy and a tiny bit trapped. She wondered if the woman wore contacts or had some kind of...eye magic.

"No thanks," she said. "I'm just waiting for my friend."

"I'll read your cards for free," said the woman. "You've got an intriguing aura." She closed her eyes and drew in a deep breath. "Fear and desperation. But also disobedience. And fierce passion." The woman's lip curled, revealing broken teeth. Her yellow eyes snapped open, and Maren flinched. "Such strong emotions for a child. I'd love to know more about you."

If Maren had a list of things she'd love to do, getting to know this woman would be dead last on it. "Umm. Maybe another time."

Before the woman could answer, she dashed away. At the end of the row of tents stood a little blue booth with a teapot painted on the side. It belonged to Beverly Thomas, who sold ten flavors of loose-leaf tea. If you brought your empty paper cup back to Beverly, she'd read your fortune. But the booth was empty, all of the tea-making equipment gone.

COMING SOON: BITTERBLACK BREWS, read a silver and black card taped to the counter.

Maren shivered despite the warm sunlight. Everything felt wrong at this end of the pier. Everything was starting to feel wrong in Rockpool Bay.

A faint buzz behind her head sent a jolt of panic through Maren's veins. She froze as the buzzing grew louder and something brushed her hair, then her earlobe.

A bee.

Don't move, she told herself, sweat instantly soaking the back of her shirt. *All you have to do is stand still and it will go away. It doesn't want to sting you.*

Unless it's a wasp, in which case it doesn't care if it stings you because it won't die. But you might.

Maren held her breath, waiting for the bee—or the wasp—to get bored and go away. Instead, it flitted to her shoulder and crawled down her sleeve. She swallowed a scream, because a scream would definitely scare the dangerous little insect.

"Don't move." Amos's voice behind her was calm. He slid a napkin between the bee and Maren's arm, then carefully shooed it away into the salty sunshine. Maren took a great, gasping gulp of air, sagging as the oxygen returned to her brain.

"Thank you."

"No problem." A smattering of sprinkles flashed on the front of Amos's shirt. He gave Maren a crooked grin. "I didn't want to have to go back to the hospital again today."

"I have my EpiPen," she said huffily, but she almost wanted to hug him. Almost. She double-checked her backpack pocket to make sure the EpiPen was still there, even though she never took it out. "Are you ready to collect ingredients now?"

"Yes."

"Try to keep up, because the tide's coming in." Maren slipped between two tents and ducked under the pier's railing.

"Where are we going?" said Amos, catching hold of the rail and looking warily at the drop to the rocks below.

Maren pointed to a rusty ladder that ran down one of the pier's thick wooden posts and ended in shadows. "Where the nightmare stuff is."

———

Amos edged around a barnacle-crusted boulder and leapt over a dead seagull covered in muck.

"This is *not* what I was expecting when you said we were going to the pier," he said.

Chattering voices and lilting organ music filtered down through the boards overhead, but underneath the pier was a different universe. Everything echoed wrong in the dim light, and it stank of decay and seaweed.

"What do you need?" said Amos.

Maren rubbed her jaw and thought. One of the nightmares could be about a sinking submarine. "Water," she said.

"Want me to get it?"

"Sure." Maren found a small plastic container in her backpack and gave it to Amos. She pointed to a sloshing, dark pool. "Try to get some from there, where it's extra scummy." Tiny details like that made the dreams extra vibrant. Done correctly, the taste of that water scum would stick with someone halfway through their morning. Maren would only add one-tenth the usual amount, and she planned to include a few safety elements like a flashlight and a diving helmet. The dreams had to be scary enough to count as nightmares, but they needed to leave people with a sense of safety and well-being.

As for the whispering dust, she'd tell Obscura she'd tried and failed again to get it from the safe. It wouldn't work as an excuse forever, but it would buy time.

Amos returned with his jeans wet up to the knees, but he held up the container proudly. The water inside had a green-grayish hue, with little chunks of foam floating on top. Maren would need to boil it first to make it safe to consume, but the essence would remain.

"That's perfect." She stowed it away in her bag.

"So are you going to tell me what's going on with that lady?" said Amos.

Maren sighed and made her way into the dark under-belly of the pier, where the rotten seaweed stench grew so strong she could taste it. "She's a customer from the dream shop. She had some…special requests, and I'm making them for her."

"Then what's she doing at the hospital? Why isn't she talking to you about it at the store?" Amos's sneaker slurped into something marshy, and he leapt sideways with a squeak.

"Because Gran-Gran can't know about it," said Maren. "Can you reach that?" She pointed up into the dripping shadows.

"The spider? I can't see if it's…"

"No, just the web." Maren wished she'd brought a flashlight, but Amos pulled out his phone and shone light into a gap between two slimy posts, where a gauzy web stretched. "There." She pointed to the edge of the web.

Back when Amos lived on Maren's street, they were the same height, but now he was a few inches taller. He stood on tiptoe and stretched. "Yeah, I can reach it."

"Hang on." Maren rummaged in her bag and pulled out a pair of nail scissors. "This way you don't have to pull the whole web down—and the spider with it." She shuddered and took a step back as Amos clipped the corner of the web, then held out a baggie for him to drop it into.

A new dream took shape in Maren's mind, one where the dreamer got caught in a huge web. After a few frightful moments, she'd make the silk cocoon turn into a sleeping bag.

"Why can't you tell your Gran what you're doing?"

"Nobody can know," said Maren, though she wished she could tell just one person who was conscious. "Sorry."

"Is it bad?" Amos's cheek caught a sliver of light that

slipped through the pier. His expression was so kind and concerned, Maren had a hard time believing this was the same person who'd defended the meanest boy at school.

"Sort of," she whispered.

"I knew it." Amos's eyes flashed with anger. "Why don't you tell your parents? Or the police?"

"Because if I do, she'll tell them something terrible I did." A sob caught in Maren's chest. She'd been so sure that telling someone would make her feel better, but it just made the situation clearer. She turned away and picked up an empty plastic soda bottle, not for a dream, but to recycle it when they went back.

"How terrible could it be?" said Amos. "You didn't kill anybody, right?"

"No." Maren blinked her tears away. "But if I tell, other people will be in trouble, too."

"That stinks," said Amos. "But if you do decide to tell and you want somebody to be there with you, let me know."

Maren's laugh came out barbed. "Right, because you've done such a great job of standing with me in the past."

Amos had the grace to look away. "I never wanted to hurt you. But you cut me off and I didn't know what I was supposed to do."

Maren stepped over a half-submerged, rotting beam. "You were supposed to choose me. Not Curtis."

Amos's betrayal seemed like such a small problem compared to the gargantuan catastrophe she faced now. But it wasn't nothing.

"I wish I had," said Amos. "I'm sorry."

"The only way I'll accept your apology is if you *do* something the next time he starts harassing somebody," said Maren. "Not just me. If you don't, then you're just as bad as him."

Amos nodded. "I swear I won't let him get away with that stuff anymore. If you're willing to hang out with me again, I promise to be a better friend. My mom misses you, too. She keeps nagging me to invite you over for dinner."

Maren's lips twitched toward a smile, even though she hadn't completely forgiven him. Maybe one day this would all be over and she'd have dinner at Amos's house like a normal person. "I'll think about it."

"I'll even volunteer to test out these nightmares for you," said Amos. "To prove how serious I am."

Maren laughed. Amos hated nightmares even more than she did. "I appreciate that, but it's not necessary."

"Okay, well the offer's out there if you change your mind." Amos put on a serious face and held out his hand, which Maren shook with her muddy one. For the first time in a long while, her chest glowed warm.

Seventeen

THE NEXT MORNING WAS FRIDAY. Six days until Hallie moved to the long-term facility. Maren had been up until nearly four a.m., mixing and boiling and microwaving her sinister ingredients, then measuring them out into her parents' electric coffee grinder. She'd snuck it into the garage so the noise of the machine wouldn't wake them. Now she was groggy and her head ached, but the nightmares were done. Hopefully they were scary enough to satisfy Obscura, but safe enough at the end to soothe the dreamers.

Sluggish and clumsy, Maren climbed aboard the starry starfish bus and dropped her quarters into the slot.

"Ahoy, Miss Partridge," called a rusty old voice from the back. Captain Perry waved and patted the empty seat beside him, and Maren took it.

"Are you going to the hospital, too?" she asked, hoping he wouldn't run into Obscura if he was.

"No, I'm headed to the hardware store," said Captain Perry. "Boat needs a few minor repairs."

Maren breathed a quiet sigh of relief. "Is your truck still in the shop?"

"I haven't driven since the accident," said Perry. "Figured it might be time for me to slow down a little."

"Oh, I'm sorry." Maren didn't know why she was apologizing when he'd been the one to hit her, but she still felt bad for him.

"That's all right." Captain Perry gave her a wrinkly wink. "Gives me time to appreciate the lovely scenery. When you're old like me, you'll appreciate it, too."

They sat, quietly appreciating the scenery together, as the bus groaned and strained down Main Street. Maisie Mae's was still closed, and so was the grocery store.

"Haven't they gotten rid of the wasps?" asked Maren, unzipping the EpiPen compartment of her backpack and running her finger over its plastic top.

Captain Perry shook his head. "They sprayed the rosebush with all kinds of stuff, but those blasted bugs won't budge. The board of health told Ernesto he needs to cut down the whole bush if he wants to reopen, but he told 'em to get scuppered."

Maren couldn't begin to imagine the Green and Fresh without that beautiful bush and the sweet smell of roses. At least she couldn't claim responsibility for the wasps, but it was sickening to watch her town slowly fall apart.

"Aye, it's a shame," said Captain Perry. "Things are changing around here."

Maren shivered at the echo of the spindly man's words outside the Monkey's Paw.

"My daughter wants me to move down to Florida with her," said Perry. "I keep saying no, but the cold nights are seeping into my bones. I'm hardly sleeping at all."

Maren sat up in her seat. "Hardly sleeping how, exactly? Insomnia? Waking up a lot?"

She couldn't bear to say the word, but Captain Perry said it for her:

"Nightmares. For months now, even before the accident. That's why I was so jumbled the day I hit you and your poor, wee sister. I hadn't slept more'n a wink."

Maren almost fell out of her seat. The hardware store appeared ahead, and Captain Perry started gathering up his things. Quickly, she turned to face him. "Do you remember what any of your nightmares were about?"

"Aye, I remember the one I had the night before I hit you lassies. Terribly sorry again."

Maren waved away his apology as the bus began to slow. "What was it?"

"My teeth were falling out," said Captain Perry, rubbing his jaw and shuddering. "By the handful. And they weren't just human teeth, no—there were shark teeth and horse teeth and wee, pointy rat teeth."

That was one of Hallie's nightmares, one that Lishta deemed too disgusting to sell at the store. There was only one way someone could have gotten hold of that dream: if Hallie had given it to them.

Maren's vision began to swim. No wonder Hallie had been acting so weird. Obscura must have been forcing her to steal nightmares, too, and Hallie must have been sneaking around, hiding her guilt just like Maren was doing now. Maren wondered how many nightmares her sister had stolen for Obscura, how long it had gone on.

"All right there?" Captain Perry peered at Maren. "I hope I didn't scare you just then. Figured you of all people wouldn't mind that sort of stuff."

"No, it's fine." Maren wiped her upper lip and tried to smile, though her heart thumped so loud she could barely hear. "Come by the shop later and I'll give you some dreams to help you sleep, okay?"

"That'd be much appreciated," said Captain Perry. "Say

hello to your sister. And tell her I've got a new song to play for her tomorrow."

"I will." A shrill whining sound filled Maren's ears as she watched him exit the bus.

And then it hit her like a load of wet cement: If Captain Perry hadn't been so tired from Obscura giving him nightmares and Hallie hadn't been so distracted by what she was doing for Obscura, maybe they both would have paid attention at that traffic light. Maybe the accident would never have happened.

Maren's entire body began to shake.

Obscura was the reason she'd lost her sister. Maren might be a nightmare thief, but Obscura was a sister thief. And she hadn't even stopped when Hallie nearly died; she just moved on to the next sister like it was nothing. The Partridges *were* nothing to her, just pawns to get whatever she wanted. Maren balled her hands into fists, so tight her nails dug into the skin, and squeezed until her trembling limbs stilled.

She was done being a pawn.

It was time to put an end to this nightmare.

Eighteen

MAREN STORMED ACROSS THE HOSPITAL parking lot, fists clenched, jaw clenched, eyes screwed up against the stinging, silvery rain that had begun to fall as soon as she got off the bus. The usual meeting spot was empty, and a steady stream of visitors filtered in and out of the swishing front doors.

"Where are you," she muttered, stalking back and forth across the curb.

"Hello, precious," came a voice from behind her.

Maren jumped, stifling a yelp, and spun around.

Obscura looked like she'd wandered straight out of the 1930s, in a pearl-colored skirt, matching jacket, and a pillbox hat with a mesh veil that came down over her eyes. Above the veil perched a black moth with the white outline of a skull on its back. Maren stuck her fists in her pockets and tried to look strong as she followed the woman around the side of the building.

Obscura licked her plum-colored lips. "Have you brought my treasures?"

Maren couldn't quite read her eyes under the veil, but there was something feline in her expression. Like a cat who'd caught a mouse and was batting it around, tiring it out before killing it. Or so Obscura thought.

"What is *wrong* with you?" said Maren.

The smile on Obscura's painted lips didn't budge. "Excuse me?"

"You blackmailed my sister. And she's in this hospital because of you. She almost died."

Obscura scoffed. "I'd say she's in this hospital because of her bad driving."

Maren threw herself at the woman, who sidestepped her neatly and flung her onto the curb.

"Don't try that again." Obscura's quiet voice sent chills down Maren's spine.

"It's over," said Maren, gasping to find the breath that'd been knocked out of her. "I'm done giving you dreams."

Obscura leaned in close, and the cloying scent of her jasmine perfume made Maren want to sneeze. "Of course it's not over. I've barely gotten started."

"Well, you'll have to figure out another way." Maren ignored her nervous feet, which desperately wanted to jump up and run away.

"Have you forgotten our deal?" Obscura held up her phone. "I've got the emails queued up and ready to send. The videos are uploaded, and I just need to push a button."

"Go ahead and do it," said Maren. "I don't care anymore." No punishment from Lishta or the doctors or the whole town of Rockpool Bay could be worse than continuing this repulsive scheme that had destroyed Hallie's life. It was only a matter of time before something similar happened to another victim.

Obscura was on her in a flash, her fingernails digging into Maren's forearm, her hot, angry mouth inches from her ear. "You little fool. Do you really think you can just walk away from this?"

Maren sucked in a breath, not sure if she should scream or fight back. Or both.

"Hey!" came Amos's voice from across the parking lot. "What are you doing?"

The woman's talons released, and Maren leapt up. "Come on!" she yelled as she ran. Without a second's hesitation, Amos dashed after her. Maren didn't look back; she didn't hear the click-clack of Obscura's shoes, but it didn't mean they were safe. She grabbed Amos's sleeve and pointed at a lone taxi idling beside the bus stop.

"Do you have money?" she gasped as they splashed through puddles and dodged around slow-moving visitors clutching flower arrangements and balloons.

"Yeah."

"Good, because I've only got quarters." As they skidded to a stop by the cab, Maren finally looked back. No sign of Obscura, which was somehow scarier than her chasing them. Amos tugged the taxi's door open and let Maren climb in first. "Can you take us to the typewriter store just off Main Street?" she said to the driver. "Quickly?"

"You got it." The driver hit the gas before Maren had time to find her seat belt. As the cab zoomed out onto the street— into traffic where any number of cars could smash right into them—Maren's heart punched her ribs as she stuck her hand into the seat crack, rummaging through crumbs and trash and God knew what else, but she couldn't find the seat belt buckle.

"Here." Amos held up the belt for the middle seat, and Maren slid over. With her seat belt clicked and pulled tight, she could breathe again, though the taxi tore along at a speed that made her want to shut her eyes. She pulled out her phone and called Lishta, but there was no answer at the dream shop, and her cell phone went straight to voicemail.

"Are you going to tell me what's going on?" said Amos.

"It's over." Maren tapped out a text message:

I'm on my way to the shop. If Ms. Malo/Obscura Gray shows up, DO NOT LET HER IN.

"What is?" said Amos.

Maren squeezed her eyes shut and took a slow breath. She could cry about this later. Right now she had to fix it. *Step toe toe heel step heel* went her stubborn foot that wasn't going to let her cry. *Step toe toe heel step heel.*

"Hey." Amos poked her arm. "What's over?"

Maren clutched her phone to her chest. "That whole situation I couldn't tell you about."

The cabdriver caught Maren's eye in the rearview mirror, and she broke off.

"Sorry to interrupt," said the driver, "but which way do you want me to go to get around the parade?"

"Around the what?" said Maren.

"Main Street's closed all day for the fishermen's festival parade." The driver flicked at the map on his dashboard-mounted phone. "We can take Steeplechase or Applewood."

"Whichever is faster," said Maren.

"Six of one, half a dozen of the other," said the driver, and Maren wanted to scream, because she didn't care how they got to the shop; it just needed to be faster than Obscura could get there.

"Applewood." Amos had his phone out, too, and the map on his screen was a web of red lines.

The driver cut a hard left. Maren gripped the seat and breathed slowly, in through her nose and out through her mouth. In and out. Everything would be okay. She just had to keep telling herself that until it was true.

Step toe toe heel step heel.

"All the way out here," the driver muttered as they rolled up to a long line of cars. He consulted his phone again, then swung them into a violent U-turn that slammed Maren's head against Amos's shoulder.

"I know we said we're in a hurry, but do you think you could slow down a little?" Amos turned to Maren. "You okay?"

"No, please keep driving like that," she said. "I have to tell Gran-Gran before *she* does."

Again, the driver's eyes met hers in the mirror, and it was probably just idle curiosity, but Maren wondered if there was more than that. For all she knew, Obscura had planted this taxi at the hospital and hired the driver to snatch her if she tried to run.

"All right, kid, be honest with me now," said the driver, and for a moment Maren thought he was about to reveal he was in cahoots with Obscura, but then he continued: "How big of an emergency is this?"

"Massive," she said. "Colossal."

"*Titanic*-sized," added Amos, though he had no idea.

"All right then." The driver bumped two wheels up over the sidewalk and steered around a roadblock barrier. Main Street swarmed with damp tourists, costumed performers on stilts, and heart-stoppingly daring acrobats. Maren's heart sank down to her knees. They'd never make it through. But the driver didn't stop; he slowed to a crawl and laid on his horn.

"Watch out!" he yelled through his open window as the taxi inched into the crowd. "Coming through."

A massive float rolled past, decorated with seashells and fishing nets. On top, a band of people dressed as mermaids played guitars and keyboards. The silvery rain gave their scaly costumes an extra sparkle. Behind the float, a troupe of pirate-clowns jogged and skipped, juggling plastic cutlasses and handing out chocolate coins.

In one smooth motion, the taxi slipped into the parade, behind a woman wearing a rainbow wig and riding a unicycle. She blew singing bubbles into the crowd, but the mermaid band drowned out their songs.

"Smile and wave," said the driver, lowering all the windows of the taxi. "Act like we're supposed to be here."

Maren gulped down her fear and plastered a smile onto her face. Even though the yellow cab wasn't decorated for the parade, people seemed happy to wave back to her, and a few kids screamed for her to throw them candy. Confetti mingled with the shimmery rain pattering down around the car, and a purple bubble drifted in through her open window.

"Twinkle, twinkle, little star," it sang, then popped.

After ten agonizingly slow blocks of music and merriment and wet, dancing sea creatures, the cab skirted around another blockade and they were zooming again, weaving and swerving, stopping and starting. Finally, Maren recognized the blue flowerpots and multicolored shutters of the neighborhood a few blocks behind the dream shop.

"We can walk from here," she said. "Thank you so, so much for doing that."

"I don't mess around with *Titanic*-sized emergencies," said the driver.

Amos handed over some money, and they raced up a lane lined with aspen trees. As her feet thundered and splashed along the pavement, Maren prayed that they weren't too late, that Obscura had gotten stuck in the same parade roadblocks. She couldn't bear the thought of Lishta hearing that woman's warped version of the truth first. She should have confessed as soon as Obscura started threatening her. It seemed so clear now—Maren never should have let it spiral out of control like this.

The front door of the typewriter shop was locked, and the sign said CLOSED, which Maren took to be a good omen. Lishta must have gotten her text after all. She fumbled her key out of her pocket and stuck it in the lock.

The shop's dark and dusty interior smelled wonderful, as always.

"Gran-Gran?" called Maren.

A soft rummaging sound came from behind a stack of boxes, and Artax slunk out with a quiet meow. Maren brushed the dust from the cat's fur, and Amos sneezed. A gap of light shone through the half-open door to the dream shop.

"Gran-Gran?" called Maren.

No answer.

Maybe Lishta was too absorbed in her dream-making to hear. Maren wove through the tables of typewriters, dread pooling in her gut.

"Gran-Gran?"

She pushed the door open. A jumble of boxes and bins lay scattered across the counter, their contents spilled onto the floor. The coffee grinder was missing, the butter churn lay on its side, and the ladder leaned drunkenly against the sanitizer machine.

Worst of all, Lishta was gone.

Nineteen

"Gran-Gran?"

Dreams crunched under Maren's shoes as she checked behind the counter, in the typewriter stockroom, in the bathroom. She knew there was no point, but she couldn't stop searching, couldn't accept what was happening. The shop was eerily silent—Henri was missing, too.

"There's a note." Amos held up a blank dream contract with two short lines of tiny writing across the back.

1389 Sinclair Street

Tell anyone, and you'll never see her again.

Beside it lay a single hairpin. Though it was just a piece of metal, it felt like a piece of Lishta. Maren squeezed it tight inside her fist, as if this could somehow keep her grand-mother safe.

"She's got Gran-Gran," she said.

"Wait, the lady from the hospital took your gran?" Amos looked like he didn't know what to believe anymore.

"Yes," said Maren impatiently. She typed the note's address into her phone. "I need to go there right now. The 79 bus stop isn't far."

"Are you kidding?" said Amos. "We need to call the police."

Maren waved the note in Amos's face, and he flinched. "Did you not read this? She said we can't tell anybody. Amos, she is really, very scary, and I don't know what she'll do to Gran-Gran." Maren's voice came out so shrill that she had to stop and swallow a few times before continuing. "You don't have to come with me, but you can't tell anybody. You have to promise me you won't."

"I'm not going to let you go running off after some crimi-nal by yourself," said Amos. "But don't kidnappers *always* say you can't tell the cops? What makes you think you can rescue her better than they can?"

Tapping Lishta's hairpin against her nose, Maren scanned the shelves. Lots of ingredients were missing, in addition to the dreams. But the square jar full of dreamsalt sat untouched on its shelf.

"Because I have something she needs." Maren unzipped her backpack and stuck the jar inside. The safe door had been opened. At least half of the nightmares were gone, and so was the whispering dust. Maren couldn't begin to imagine the awful things Obscura might do with that dust. Shuddering, she took a paper bag, filled it with the rest of the nightmares, and folded the top closed. "Honestly, you don't have to come," she said. "But you have to let me go."

"I'm coming." Amos took the bag full of dreams and stuffed it inside his backpack. "But only if you tell me everything."

"I will," said Maren. "On the way there."

By the time the 79 bus—painted with green horses and seahorses—navigated through approximately four hundred detours and picked up roughly nine thousand festivalgoers, the rain had turned to a deluge. The windshield wipers couldn't keep up with the downpour, and the driver hunched over the steering wheel, muttering and cursing Mother Nature and pedestrians alike.

"I told my mom the first time I saw Obscura at the hospital." Maren wiped a hole in the fog on her window and peered through. They'd reached the hilly part of town now, dotted with shabbier houses and sandy soil and empty lots. "But she didn't think it was serious, and I didn't want to stress her out any more than she already was. Then I told Lishta, and she *did* think it was serious, but she's told me a million times that she'd ban me from the shop if I broke the rule. And I just kept breaking it. But what really messes me up is the fact that Hallie did the exact same thing."

Amos drummed his fingers against his knee, and Maren braced herself for the inevitable lecture about how she should have confessed everything at the beginning of this mess.

"I can't believe you're actually feeling guilty about any of this," he said finally. "Obscura's even more diabolical than I thought."

Maren sputtered. She'd been carrying the weight of this guilt for so long that she didn't know how to let go of it.

"Every step of the way, she forced you to make bad decisions," continued Amos. "She manipulated you. Both of you. There was no way you could have won."

"I wasn't trying to win," said Maren. "I just didn't want her to destroy my life. But she did anyway."

"Well she's not going to get away with it," said Amos firmly. "So what's your plan for when we get there?"

"It's changed a little bit now that you're coming," said Maren. "Here's what I'm thinking. When we get there, you'll hide while I offer to help Obscura with her dream-making scheme. Then I'll create some kind of distraction—not sure what yet. Meanwhile, you can sneak in and get Gran-Gran. Then you'll both escape and call the police and they'll come before Obscura realizes what's going on."

Amos wrinkled his nose. "What kind of distraction?"

"I don't know. Do you have any ideas?"

"Slip her a bunch of nightmares?" He nudged his bag on the floor.

"That'll be hard if she's not asleep," said Maren. "We'll have to stay flexible, but you'll be the secret weapon she doesn't see coming." She looked out through her fog hole in the window and checked her phone one last time. "This is our stop."

Twenty

As soon as Maren and Amos stepped off the bus, the hammering rain caught them, instantly soaking their clothes. Swiping water out of her eyes, Maren surveyed her surroundings. Nobody went to this part of town anymore. Tucked in a hollow between the hills, it had been a popular area for locals when Maren's mom was a kid, but over the past few decades more and more people had been unable to find year-round jobs and had left town. The businesses here had either shuttered for good or moved closer to the touristy waterfront, leaving empty parking lots and dusty shells of buildings.

The black clouds overhead were almost low enough to touch, and the wind sheared through Maren's drenched sweatshirt. Shivering, she checked the address on her phone again and pointed across the street. Between a boarded-up penny arcade and a pizza restaurant with rotting leather booths, a chain-link gate closed off a long driveway.

"There," she said.

As they crossed the road, Amos stumbled and fell to his knees. Maren helped him up, and he gave her a sheepish grin.

"Thanks." He tried to wipe the water from his jeans, but it was pointless. They were both soaked to the skin.

"Thank *you* for coming with me." Maren peered up at the imposing metal gate and shivered again. Something glinted at the foot of a post, and she stooped to pick it up. Another hairpin.

"Gran-Gran's here," she said, tucking it into her pocket.

A padlock held the gate shut tight, so she began to climb the slick fence, making sure not to look down until she was over the top and halfway down the other side. Amos climbed faster than Maren, but as he swung his leg over the top, his backpack snagged and he almost fell.

"Careful!" Maren held up her arms to catch him, but Amos would crush her if he did fall. He unhooked his bag, then climbed down much more slowly.

"Are you okay?" asked Maren.

"Yeah, just a little...winded."

Maren had seen Amos run soccer drills for hours without getting remotely winded. She crouched beside him and wiped beads of rain from his forehead. Amos's cheeks were a greenish shade of gray; he turned his head away and spat.

"What the heck is that?" he yelped, pointing to a prickly, red-berried bush in the parking lot behind the pizza place.

Maren squinted at the plant. "Japanese barberry." She'd collected the plant's thorns and berries a few times for dreams. "Why?"

"I thought it was moving." Amos shook his head as if to clear it out. "Must've been the rain."

Shading her eyes, she pointed up the driveway to a grand old building made of stone. Round-topped windows stretched up several stories on either side of a battered marquee that held no letters, just spray-painted tags and rusty stains. The windows were all smashed and boarded up, and the front of the building looked charred, like it had been in a fire.

"This is the Starlight Theater," she said. "Gran-Gran and my mom used to come to shows here, but it's been closed for something like twenty years."

Amos wasn't listening. He stood stock-still, staring at a gleaming puddle, his breath coming in short gasps.

"Hey," said Maren. "Are you having a panic attack?"

Amos's head gave a faint twitch: *no.*

"Asthma?" Amos didn't have asthma when he lived in Maren's neighborhood, but she'd heard these things could change as people got older. "Can we please try to hurry up? Gran-Gran's—"

"Shh!" Amos hissed. "I think they can hear us."

Maren glanced up at the building, but it was too far away for anyone to hear. "Who can?"

Amos raised a shaking hand and pointed at the puddle's surface, which churned with thousands of raindrops. "The people in the submarine. Look, there's the periscope!"

"That's not funny." Maren wiped the rain off her face again, grabbed his elbow, and tugged him away from the puddle. He sounded almost like he was dreaming, like he'd taken one of the submarine disaster nightmares from the shop. But she didn't understand how that was possible unless he'd been secretly taking nightmares on the bus. Which would be a really foolish thing to do.

Half dragging Amos, whose feet seemed to not want to cooperate anymore, Maren hurried toward the theater. She couldn't see with all this rain, couldn't think properly. She needed to get him somewhere dry and figure out what was wrong.

"PETITE AMIE D'UN OGRE MALODORANT!" came a screeching voice.

Maren stumbled and Amos stepped on the heel of her waterlogged shoe. "Did somebody just call you the girlfriend of a…a smelly ogre?" he said, glancing nervously around. "Is there an ogre here?"

"Henri, I never thought I'd say this, but I'm glad you're here," Maren said to the general area of trees where Henri was hiding. "Is Gran-Gran inside?"

"JOLIE MADEMOISELLE," Henri let out a furious squawk, and Amos covered his ears with his hands and began whispering to himself.

Maren looked at the crumbling old theater and shuddered. A crooked cement roof protruded from the building's facade, leaving a rectangle of dry pavement in front of the entrance. The board over the center set of doors had been shifted aside, revealing a gap of dark interior, but Maren wasn't ready to face the inside yet. She grabbed Amos's arm and dragged him, stumbling and splashing through puddles, under the shelter of the overhanging roof. He sank the ground, mumbling nervously about slugs and dentist drills, which didn't make sense if he was having the submarine nightmare.

"Let's get this off so you can lie down." Maren pulled the strap of Amos's backpack, then froze in horror. The fabric of the bag was saturated—with water on top, but with an oily black substance on the bottom.

"Oh no, no, no," whispered Maren. As she eased the bag off Amos's shoulders, inky droplets fell onto her shoes and ran onto the pavement, where they curled and slithered. The nightmares were dissolving.

She ripped open the backpack, and black liquid gushed out, its oily surface shimmering with flashes of blue and green. The stench was unimaginable: putrid food, roadkill, sewers, and blood. Maren gagged as she plunged her hands into the slippery murk, searching for sachets that hadn't yet dissolved. Her vision began to swim. She knew she shouldn't let the nightmares seep into her skin, but she needed them to bargain with Obscura. She *needed* them.

A hole opened up in the theater's wall. Stretching wider and wider, it yawned like a mouth. Maren leapt backward, spilling the contents of the backpack onto the pavement. Coils of black slithered out.

"It's just a dream, just a dream," she whispered. But she couldn't tell where the dream ended and reality started. Amos lay fast asleep on the concrete, his legs twitching and his hands swiping at things that weren't there. Guilt hit Maren like a bag of bricks. She never should have let him come, never should have told him about Obscura. There was no reason to drag him into this, other than her own fear of being alone and the fact that he'd had money for the taxi. Now he lay there suffering, and there was nothing Maren could do.

Something brushed the back of Maren's neck, and she

whirled around. A bus-sized caterpillar crouched on the pavement. Its round black eyes locked on Maren's, and its mouth opened to reveal jagged teeth the size of her hand.

"You're not real, you're not real," Maren backed slowly away until she hit the theater. She felt so tired; her eyelids weighed a hundred pounds each. Not caring that it wasn't real, the caterpillar inched toward her, reaching with its long antennae.

"Go away, bug," Maren's voice came out a squeak, and she couldn't get her hand to stop shaking as she held it up to the insect's huge, furry snout. "Shoo. *Shoo.*"

The caterpillar sprang at Maren, its jaws wide enough to swallow her head. With a scream, she covered her face.

And lurched sideways.

Someone had pulled her inside the building. It was so dark she couldn't see a thing.

"Amos," she gasped.

Someone's arm slid around her waist, urging her farther inside the building. Maren wrenched away and ran toward a rectangle of dim, gray light.

A cavernous space opened up in front of her. A theater filled with gilded chairs and wine-red carpets on a slanting floor that led to a broad stage with its velvet curtains closed. The domed ceiling was painted like a sky, and the marble columns supporting it were carved with angels and demons and fairies and monsters. As Maren ran down the aisle, the theater began to flicker, its colors washing in and out, and she caught glimpses of gray and dirt under the burgundy and brocade. Flashes of rusty pipes and wires, rotten carpet, and broken glass.

Somewhere in the theater, a piano began to play. An eerie, tinkling tune like something out of a music box in a horror movie.

"Amos!" She'd forgotten him again—she couldn't think straight. Maren whirled around and tried to run up the incline, but the carpet began to slide under her feet. It grew softer and deeper, and her feet disappeared into it. Down, down, down Maren sank until the carpet came up to her hips. At the back of the theater, two figures appeared, one holding the other up. A boy and a tall, thin woman.

"Amos!"

The carpet snuck up to Maren's chin. It trapped her arms, and her feet kicked uselessly against its scratchy softness. Down she sank until the carpet closed over her head, and she didn't know which way was up or down, and everything was scratchy and stifling.

Then it all went black.

Twenty-One

MAREN'S EYES DRIFTED OPEN. SHE sat slumped on a metal chair with her face on a table and a string of drool trailing down her cheek. The dim light hurt her eyes. Gingerly, she eased her head up and wiped crust from the corner of her lips. As her vision adjusted, her surroundings began to take shape.

The table sat at the edge of a stage, looking out over a decrepit theater that looked nothing like what Maren had seen in her nightmare haze. The few scraps of carpet that remained in the aisles were moth-eaten, and most of the wooden seats had rotted through. High overhead, the domed ceiling was dotted with holes through which gray sky showed and rain dripped. Black mold covered the carved stone pillars that held up the ceiling. In the orchestra pit, a derelict grand piano lay on its side, as if it had stage-dived off and nobody caught it. Trash littered the ground.

The stage's curtains were full of holes, and the scenery at the back had faded beyond recognition. But the stage itself was pristine. Someone had swept up every scrap of rubbish and polished its boards until they shone. Underneath the stench of mildew and dust, Maren detected a lemony hint of the floor soap her mother loved.

A rustle of movement in the wings, and Obscura swept in. She wore a black warm-up suit and pink pointe shoes. She'd gathered her dark hair into a low bun, and a black and yellow striped moth clung to her sleeve. Maren tried to jump out of her chair, but her left foot didn't budge. A plastic zip tie cinched around her ankle held it tight against the table leg.

Ignoring Maren, Obscura headed for a freestanding ballet barre in the center of the stage, set one hand on it, and dropped into a sweeping plié.

"Where are Amos and my grandmother?" said Maren.

Obscura lifted one long arm overhead, and the moth fluttered on her wrist. "Hello to you, too. And you're welcome for saving you from…whatever was threatening you outside." Her mouth twitched. "I would've expected you of all people to be a bit more careful with nightmares."

With a jolt, Maren realized her backpack had disappeared.

And so had Amos's bag. Her heart sank at the foolishness of what she'd done. She'd delivered herself and another hostage to Obscura's door and then put them both to sleep. She couldn't have made it easier if she'd tried.

"Where are they?" she repeated.

Obscura began to swing her leg to the front and back, front and back, higher and higher with each sweep. "They're around. You can see them once you've helped me for a little while."

Maren folded her arms. "I won't do anything until I know they're okay."

"They're perfectly fine." Obscura's pointed foot careened high over her head. She brought it to the floor, swiveled around so her other hand rested on the barre, and began to swing the other leg. "Make me three nightmares and I'll let you see them." Her leg still flying, she pointed to a stack of bins beside the table—Maren recognized them from the shop's storage room.

"Why are you doing this?" said Maren.

Obscura left the barre and pulled the moth from her sleeve. "Do you know what this is, my darling?" The insect let out a harsh buzzing sound that made Maren's skin crawl. "It's a hybrid species I picked up in Brazil. Scarlet tiger moth crossed with *killer bee*." Obscura held up the killer moth-bee to show Maren the two-inch-long barb on its rear end.

Maren tried to leap out of her chair and grab her backpack, but the zip tie dug into her ankle. Tutting, Obscura waggled her finger as the killer insect crawled down her knuckle.

"Please," said Maren, her throat so dry the word barely came out. "I need my EpiPen. I could die."

"Well then, you'd better listen very carefully to what I need you to do." Obscura sauntered closer, and Maren realized she had no intention of getting the EpiPen, didn't care if Maren died if she didn't get what she wanted. A bead of chilly sweat slid down the back of her T-shirt.

Obscura leaned in to whisper to the insect. "We don't like her, do we?"

Maren shrank back as far as she could in her chair, eyes watering, as the killer moth-bee's sawlike hum filled her ears. "I'll make three," she said, fighting the tremor in her voice. "Then you'll show me Gran-Gran and Amos. That's what you said."

"Now it's four." Obscura took a graceful step backward, still holding the insect aloft. "I don't like your attitude."

Maren pulled the lid off the first bin. Empty dream sachets in various colors lay scattered among mint leaves, cigarette butts, splinters of plastic, candle ends, metal screws, a paper coffee cup, a book of matches, and a handful of dead ladybugs. Obscura must have thrown everything she could find inside, because Lishta would never have been so sloppy.

Maren's foot began to tap a fast, nervous rhythm. "Did you bring the coffee grinder?" she said.

"It's in there." Obscura set the killer moth-bee on her shoulder and returned to the barre.

"And I'll need my backpack," said Maren. "There's a jar of something important in there." Maybe she could grab her EpiPen and her phone while pretending to search for the dreamsalt.

"I already took it out for you." Obscura pointed beside one of the bins, and Maren's heart sank as she spotted the square glass jar. She must have taken her phone and EpiPen, too.

"Why isn't my grandmother making dreams for you?" said Maren.

"She's even less cooperative than you are." Obscura rose to the tips of her toes and floated across the stage. "Though I'm sure her dreams are far superior."

The insult hurt, though Maren knew that Lishta had sixty more years of practice than she did. She had a sudden urge to make the worst, most hideous nightmare ever crafted, just to prove Obscura wrong.

From the bin, she pulled out four sachets, a bag of stinging nettles, and the coffee grinder. As she plunged her hands into the scrambled contents of a second bin, something sharp pierced her fingertip. Still thinking of bees, Maren screamed. She yanked her hand out and found two thin lines of red blooming on her right index finger. Not bee stings, thank the stars. Just some kind of sharp blade.

Using her left hand, Maren opened up the black sachets, then held her bleeding finger over each one and squeezed until a droplet fell. Then she turned back to the bin, carefully lifting items out until she found the thing that had pricked her. It was a pink razor with rusted blades. Maren snapped the head off the razor and dropped it into the coffee grinder. This was going to be a painful dream.

It took a lot of effort to turn the coffee grinder's crank with the razor blades inside, and they made an awful crunching sound. On the stage, Obscura whirled and leapt and spun like a symphony spurred her on. The killer moth-bee remained motionless on her shoulder.

Once the razor blades had reached a powdery consistency, Maren opened the coffee grinder's drawer, scooped four equal portions of the nightmare mix into the black sachets, added a granule of dreamsalt to each, and blew on them before sewing them up. They'd have to do without being sterilized.

"Done," she said, pushing the nightmares across the table. "Now show me my grandmother and Amos."

Mid-lunge, Obscura narrowed her eyes.

"Please," added Maren with as much humbleness as she could muster.

Obscura finished with a triple pirouette, then sat down on the edge of the stage to remove her pointe shoes. Her feet were gnarled like an old woman's, with a red lump on the middle knuckle of each toe. One of her big toenails was blue and the rest were yellow and cracked. Maren couldn't help but think that Obscura's nail clippings would make a fantastic nightmare ingredient, though the idea of collecting them made her queasy.

Obscura stepped into a pair of high-heeled shoes and rummaged through her duffel bag. Maren glimpsed three cell phones inside and recognized the shiny red cover of her own, but then they disappeared into the bag again. The killer moth-bee left Obscura's shoulder and drifted toward Maren, letting out its awful hum. She glanced at her faraway backpack, wanting to throw up.

Obscura pulled Lishta's sharp pair of silver scissors from her bag and crouched beside the table. As she cut the zip tie on Maren's ankle, Maren cringed at the cold metal on her skin. With a flick of her finger, the ballerina sent her killer moth-bee zooming to the back of Maren's head, where it hovered, faintly brushing her hair.

"Get up," Obscura said, pointing to a door in the wings. "That way."

Maren moved slowly, trying to think of a way to escape. She could slam the door shut just as Obscura came through and possibly run, but that moth-bee could probably fit under-neath it and chase her down.

"Just be aware," came Obscura's chilly voice, accompanied by the angry buzz of her trained insect. "I won't tolerate any nonsense."

Shakily, Maren opened the door and the buzzing grew softer as she stepped through it into a dark stairwell.

"Down," ordered Obscura, and Maren clung to the banis-ter as she descended. They turned onto another hall, wet and slick and reeking of mold. From inside the walls came the tiny scratchings of rodents or cockroaches—or both.

"Stop," said Obscura.

The flashlight went out, and darkness closed like a mouth around Maren.

Bzzzzzzzzzz.

She drew a deep, shuddering breath full of mildew and fear.

A key clicked in a lock and a door swung open, bathing the hall in gray-green light. Obscura gave Maren a hard nudge, and she shuffled forward into the small space. A mirror ringed with blown-out bulbs hung over a dressing table, and along the opposite wall a tiny woman lay curled up on a cot. It took Maren a few seconds to recognize Lishta—she seemed to have shrunk since Maren had last seen her.

"Gran-Gran?" Maren's voice croaked out.

"She won't hear you," said Obscura, and Maren's blood went cold. She stopped short of Lishta's hunched form, afraid to touch her.

Obscura let out a huff of a laugh. "She's not dead, little fool. I gave her sleeping medicine."

"Gran-Gran," whispered Maren, sinking down beside the bed. "I'm here, and everything's going to be okay. They're probably looking for us already."

"That's doubtful," said Obscura. "I texted your mother from your grandmother's phone and asked if you could stay with her for the weekend. She said that was fine. Then a little while later, I texted her from your phone and told her you were having an *awesome* time."

Maren face blazed hot. She turned back to Lishta, whose eyebrows were knitted together. Her papery lips moved, but no sound came out.

"You can't keep her asleep forever," said Maren. "She's old. It can't be good for her."

Obscura shrugged. "Let's see how well you make dreams for me."

A claw closed around Maren's wrist, and she let out a shriek. But it wasn't Obscura grabbing her; it was Lishta. The old woman's head lifted up and her eyes opened so wide that Maren could see the whites all around her blue irises.

"Don't—help—her." Lishta forced each word out, then fell back onto her pillow, her lips still moving silently.

Obscura tutted. "Go stand over there," she said to Maren, pointing at the dressing table. When Maren hesitated, she gave the killer moth-bee a little flick, and it zoomed toward her. "*Now.*"

Maren leapt out of the way, and the moth-bee hovered motionless, waiting for Obscura's next command. The tall ballerina pulled an eyedropper full of clear liquid from her duffel bag and slipped it into the corner of Lishta's still-moving mouth. Then she took out one of the black sachets that Maren had just made.

"No!" It took a massive effort not to snatch the dream from her hand. Maren's insides squirmed as Obscura tucked the nightmare under Lishta's tongue. Maren shut her eyes. She couldn't watch Lishta suffer the horrible stings she knew were coming, over and over and over.

"Is this what I think it is?" Obscura pulled a small tin from her pocket and slid open its lid, her dark eyes gleaming with greed.

Maren couldn't look directly at the tin. "I have no idea what you mean."

"I think you do," said Obscura. "Gran-Gran *really* didn't want me to take it."

Maren hated, hated, hated Obscura calling Lishta

that, like she was her grandmother, too. "I've never seen it before," she said.

Obscura slid the lid one way, then the other. "You're lying."

"I'm not." Maren hid her sweating hands behind her back and tried to keep her face as unexpressive as possible.

"You have one chance to tell me," said Obscura. "Then I'm going to give some to Gran-Gran, and if you've been lying, I'll feed her the whole bottle of sleeping medicine." Obscura leaned over the sleeping woman and brushed a strand of gray hair off her forehead. "It might not kill her, but then again, it might."

Maren's stomach flopped like a fish on a hook. Lishta would die without ever waking if she didn't tell the truth. And Maren would watch it happen.

"It's whispering dust." Guilt slithered like worms over her skin. She'd promised Lishta never to tell, and now she'd just given Obscura even more ammunition.

Obscura's mouth stretched into a wicked grin. "Now show me how it works." She swiped her thumb into the tin.

"Just a tiny pinch." Maren hated herself for sharing this information, for letting Obscura know a single thing about this beautiful and dangerous ingredient Lishta had discovered.

Obscura dropped a few grains of whispering dust into Maren's palm, and Maren propped Lishta's mouth open. "I'm sorry," she whispered as she tipped it inside. Lishta shifted and muttered and went still.

"Go on." Obscura gave Maren's shoulder an impatient shove.

"Gran-Gran?" said Maren. "Can you hear me?"

"Maren?" Lishta's voice was startlingly lucid. "Is that you, sweetheart? Watch out for the stinging nettles. They're trying to catch us."

"I'll be careful," said Maren.

Lishta let out a little cry and clutched her arm, then her chest. "They're so angry. Oh, sweetheart, you'd better run. My arm is stuck, so they'll get me instead." She swatted at her face and neck and hands. "Run, Maren!"

Tears sprang to Maren's eyes. Her grandmother was trapped in a nightmare she'd made. Obscura elbowed her out of the way and bent over the old woman's ear.

"The thorns are as big as knitting needles," she whispered.

Lishta's frail body twitched, and she flung both arms over her face. "Run, sweetheart! Get out of here!"

Maren turned away, but she could still hear her grandmother's panting breath, her gasps and cries. "Where is Amos?" she said, hating herself for wanting to leave, but she couldn't, *couldn't* stay for any more of this.

Obscura gestured at the wall behind Maren. "Next door."

Maren kept her eyes averted from her grandmother. "Can I see him?"

A triumphant leer slid across Obscura's lips as she inclined her head toward the door. "After you."

In an identical dressing room next to Lishta's, Amos lay fast asleep.

"I read his text messages and figured out he was supposed to stay at a friend's house for the weekend," said Obscura. "So I texted his mother and said he was heading to his friend's, then texted his friend to say he was sick and couldn't come." Her face fell into a fake little pout. "It's rather irritating that you brought him along. Now I've got to take care of all three of you."

Take care of could mean two very different things, and Maren didn't think Obscura meant the good one. On trembling legs, she crossed the room and checked to make sure Amos was breathing. She hadn't really expected that his mom would connect his disappearance with hers, but it was unthinkable that not a single person would start looking for either one of them until Sunday night. Maren backed away from Amos before Obscura got any ideas about giving him nightmares or whispering dust.

Radiating smugness, Obscura followed her out into the dark hall. She didn't turn the flashlight back on.

"Now you see, Maren Eloise." Her whisper was sharp as knives. "You really are mine."

The wave of understanding, of horror, of sheer alone-ness nearly knocked Maren to her knees. If nobody started searching for them until Sunday, that meant at least two nights in this awful old theater. It meant at least two days of making nightmares, of appeasing Obscura so she wouldn't hurt Amos or Lishta, of not getting stung by that hideous moth-bee. Maren didn't know how she'd manage, but surviving was her only option. She had to do it for Amos and Lishta. She coughed and tried to clear the terror out of her throat.

"I'm ready to make more dreams," she said.

Twenty-Two

OBSCURA WAS BACK IN HER pointe shoes, repeating the same dance sequence over and over and over. A series of quick, hopping steps into a string of dizzying turns that traveled all the way across the stage. It looked perfect to Maren, who had finished fifty-seven nightmares so far, but Obscura had grown increasingly frustrated and had started swearing each time she finished the third turn in the sequence.

"Supposed to be a triple," she muttered, stalking back to the opposite side of the stage with her hands on her hips. She had stripped off her warm-up suit and now wore a black leotard and tights.

Maren wondered if she'd make it to her own dance class on Tuesday. There were only three rehearsals left before the recital. It seemed like a silly thing to worry about, considering her entire life was in danger, but Maren's brain had kicked into worry overdrive.

"Is that one of your old solos?" she said.

Obscura didn't answer; she was halfway across the stage again, arms whirring. The moth perched on top of her bun now. Maybe it was asleep. Maren set down her needle and wiped her trembling hands on her jeans. She hoped Lishta's nightmare had ended by now, and she'd slipped into an empty, calm sleep.

After two more repetitions, each ending like all the others, Obscura let out an angry howl and stalked to the front of the stage, where she pulled a water bottle from her bag.

Keeping her face carefully neutral, Maren tied off a knot of thread and clipped it with scissors. "If you bring your left shoulder around a little quicker, I think you'll be able to do a triple."

Obscura's eyes widened. She set her water bottle down and wiped her mouth on her wrist. Without a word, she jogged to the back of the stage and started again. This time, her triple pirouette was flawless. Maren wondered how a person who did such beautiful things with her body could have such an ugly heart. Obscura repeated the perfect sequence two more times, then leaned on the edge of Maren's table, her hand planted beside a pile of crow feathers.

"What do you know about ballet?" she said.

"Not as much as you." Maren sprinkled a pinch of cayenne onto a scrap of leather saturated with motor oil. "But I've been taking classes since I was little. Tap is my specialty."

"*Tap.*" Obscura scoffed and sat down to stretch. "Why even bother?"

Maren shrugged.

"Can you act?" said Obscura. "Or sing?"

"Not really." Maren dropped the leather strip into the coffee grinder.

"So you have no plans to ever be on Broadway, but you take *tap-dancing* lessons anyway?" Obscura twisted into a split and lay all the way forward onto her leg.

"It's fun," said Maren.

The crunching crackle of the coffee grinder drowned out Obscura's nasty commentary. Once the ingredients were all the right texture, Maren tipped everything onto the table.

"Is that really all you do?" said Obscura. "Mix nasty things in the coffee grinder and sew them into the little bags?"

"There's more to it than that," said Maren, giving a defiant *shuffle step* under the table. "You have to know the right proportions, the things that will become events in the dream and the things that just create setting or atmosphere. You need dreamsalt, and you need to have dream magic to make the dreamsalt work."

"But if I took a handful of disgusting things and made you or your grandmother blow on that salt, it'd create some kind of nightmare, would it not?" Obscura stood, eyeing the mostly gruesome ingredients scattered across the table.

Maren didn't want her to think she was expendable, so she chose her words carefully. "It'd give you a sort-of bad dream, but it'd probably be all jumbled and not have much effect." She cast a sideways glance at Obscura. "It wouldn't be *real* art."

Obscura leaned her elbows on the table and gave Maren a saccharine smile that turned her stomach. "You could teach me, though."

And then you'd have no need for me, and I would become disposable, thought Maren. "It takes a long time to learn," she said. "I've been practicing for ages now, and my dreams are still clunky."

But Obscura had already leapt down into the orchestra pit, where she found a metal folding chair and hefted it onto the stage. "I've spent twenty-five years perfecting my ballet technique. Practice doesn't scare me."

Maren fought down the panic welling in her chest. She only had to hold out for two days, maybe three. The police knew how to track people using the tiniest of clues. Someone was bound to rescue them; somebody had to have seen them getting off the bus, and maybe Henri was still squawking around outside. And two or three days was nowhere near enough time for Obscura to fully learn how to make dreams. She just had to survive that time and keep Lishta and Amos safe too.

"Okay," Maren said. "We'll start simple. Let's pick through this soil and find all the blackest grains."

It was cemetery dirt and didn't need separating, but it would buy time. Obscura pulled her chair up close, and Maren gave her the tweezers, a pair of drugstore reading glasses to magnify her work, and a plate to collect the black grains of sand on. Obscura worked quickly, humming a little as she picked through the dirt.

Maren craned her neck to see the duffel bag on the floor behind Obscura. If she could just reach one of the cell phones inside, all she needed to do was call 911 and they'd trace the call even if she didn't speak. She knew it'd work because once she'd accidentally called the number and then not answered when they called back, only to discover a police officer at her front door five minutes later.

"How did you get inside those people's houses to give them the nightmares?" said Maren.

"I didn't." Obscura set her tweezers down, and Maren's gut lurched as she pulled the killer moth-bee from her hair. She reached for a finished nightmare and held it out to the insect, which tested the sachet with its long antennae and then took it with its front legs. Maren watched, sickened and spellbound, as Obscura whispered to the moth, then pointed at her.

"Pretend you're asleep," ordered Obscura.

"I don't want to—" began Maren, but Obscura waved her hand impatiently.

"Close your eyes. *Now.*"

Maren dropped her chin to her chest and shut her eyes. Seconds later, the moth-bee's buzz grew so loud that Maren's entire body broke out in cold sweat. A quivering brush of wings on her forehead, and then the bug began to crawl down her cheek. She wanted to swat it away so badly that she had to tuck her hands under her legs. One sting and she'd swell up like a balloon and suffocate. The insect's little, tickling feet found her lips, and Maren gagged.

"Don't you dare move," said Obscura. Tears filled Maren's eyes as the moth-bee pushed the sachet into her mouth and the sour, black taste of it began to seep onto her tongue. Then the creature was gone, and Obscura was laughing. Maren spat the dream onto the table, then spat and spat again onto a paper towel until her gray spit cleared. In the corners of her vision, dark things twitched and crept.

"Why don't you finish sorting this dirt and let me know when it's done?" Obscura pushed her chair back and returned to the ballet barre. The moth-bee flitted back to her hair, and slowly, Maren's heartbeat and breathing returned to normal.

Obscura propped her long leg up on the barre. "Did you know that I grew up in Rockpool Bay?"

Maren nodded. "My grandmother said you came into the shop once when you were younger."

"So she does remember." Obscura flexed and pointed her foot as she leaned over it. "Did she tell you how she refused to help me?"

Maren picked up the tweezers and pretended to sort through the grains of cemetery dirt, keeping one eye on the duffel bag. "She told me she wouldn't give you a nightmare for revenge. She wanted to help you in a different way."

Obscura scoffed. "That wasn't helping. That was letting my brother get away with everything. He thought it was funny! Do you have any idea what it's like to be terrified to go to sleep every single night? To have those images loop endlessly through your mind all day?"

"I do, actually," said Maren.

Obscura's thin arm curved over her head as she leaned into a deep backbend. "Your grandmother thought she could patch me up with some minty relaxation dreams, but they wouldn't even scratch the surface."

Maren reached all the way across the table for the pile

of crow feathers, which she didn't need, just to see if Obscura would notice.

"With a single dream, my brother took control of my brain," continued Obscura, oblivious. "One tiny, vile nightmare that crawled into my brain and hid there permanently. Every night, it ssslithered back out."

She lifted her leg off the barre, swung it all the way around at ear height, and snapped it down into a neat fifth position. Then she left the barre and strode backstage. Maren slowly eased around the side of the table and slid into Obscura's chair.

A rusty creaking sound came from the darkness and the ballerina emerged, pushing an antique movie projector on a cart. Levers and wheels and rods stuck out at all angles from the machinery. She wheeled the projector to the front of the stage and angled it at a blank screen that hung across the backdrop.

"I'm going to renovate this place and reopen it," said Obscura. "But it won't be called the Starlight anymore. It will be the Shadow Theater, and I will be the star."

Twenty-Three

THE PROJECTOR'S LIGHT CLICKED ON; it began to tick and whirl, throwing a tangle of shadows onto the white screen. Obscura lifted to the tips of her toes and floated toward the screen. On the cart, two mechanized arms moved black cutouts in front of the projected light. The jumble of shadows on the screen shifted in and out of focus, then became clear: a puppet boy and a row of crooked buildings with a pier at the end.

"The performances will be like nothing anyone has ever seen," said Obscura. "A dark blending of shadows and dance, puppets and live performers, beauty and terror."

She flitted into the light and her shadow joined the others. It warped and stretched, bending disturbingly in places that real bodies didn't bend.

"Can you imagine what it's like to be a child with *moth*

magic in sparkly, whimsical Rockpool Bay?" said Obscura. "To be a child who whispers to bugs in a place full of enchanted ice cream and charmed candy and grocery stores full of flowers?"

As she moved away from the projector, her shadow began to shrink; her arms and legs grew shorter until she was the same size as the shadow boy. "The people in this town only value one brand of magic: it's happy and fluffy and saccharine sweet. Anybody who doesn't fit that brand is a freak. Even my own parents found my abilities unsettling."

There was an element of truth to Obscura's words, Maren thought. The cheerful magic definitely got more attention and community support. She couldn't think of any other business besides the dream shop that traded in darker areas of magic. And their nightmare dealings were always done very quietly, never advertised to tourists like everything else.

"And then my brother gave me that nightmare," said Obscura.

On-screen, a huge snake appeared, rearing up and opening its jaws, and little shadow Obscura shrank back, cowering. As the serpent grabbed her foot and began to swallow, the boy puppet laughed, clutching his stomach with glee.

"My brother thought it was hilarious. He told his friends, and they helped him continue the prank in my waking life, too. Soon the whole school was in on it." She let out a disgusted huff. "This town may look sugary sweet, but underneath that candy coating, it's rotten."

The shadow snake swallowed, gulping down the girl's leg. More child-sized puppets appeared beside the brother, pointing and jeering.

"I begged my mother to let me transfer to a different school." Obscura's voice went low and flat. "But she was too *busy* to drive me."

Maren remembered begging her own mother to let her transfer to a new school. She knew exactly how it felt to have kids whispering about her, laughing at her. Some days, it took all of her strength not to run out of school and never stop running. As much as she didn't want to, Maren felt a little bit bad for Obscura.

"By the end of sixth grade, I didn't have a single friend left," said Obscura. "Only my winged beauties stayed."

A dancing flock of shadow moths circled Obscura's head, dipping in to kiss her cheeks and perch on her shoulders. The little puppet girl grew taller. Thinner. Sharper. Her hands curled into claws.

"My only escape was the dance studio," said Obscura, and once again Maren found herself identifying with the evil woman. "I spent every day there, working on my technique. I swore I'd find a way to make people appreciate me. Respect me. Love me. When I turned fourteen, I auditioned for all the best ballet schools in the world, and I chose the one that was farthest away from this awful place."

It wasn't an awful place, but Maren didn't want to call attention to herself. If she leaned all the way back, she could almost touch the top edge of the duffel bag. Her fingers grazed the zipper.

"I worked my way up through the school, practicing day and night until I was better than every other girl there." Shadow Obscura stood at a ballet barre and swept her pointed foot back and forth. "Then I joined the company and worked and worked until I was a soloist, then a principal dancer. A prima ballerina, if you will." Her shadow swept into a deep curtesy as long-stemmed roses fell all around her. "Finally, everyone loved me. In every city we visited, I was mobbed by adoring fans. My Odette-Odile in *Swan Lake* brought entire theaters to tears."

The ballerina turned suddenly, light dancing across her face and glinting unnervingly in her eyes. Maren whipped forward in her chair. Her cheeks hot, her chest heaving, she held up the bottle of squid ink and pretended to read its label.

"That sounds nice," she said as calmly as possible.

"It was," said Obscura. "Except that I still kept having that nightmare. You can't imagine what that kind of horror, night after night, does to you. I tried keeping myself awake, but it was impossible to keep up with a touring schedule without resting. Even for someone as strong as me."

Shadow Obscura spun on one foot, whipping the other leg to propel her. Around and around she went, until suddenly her bottom leg cracked and bent the wrong way and she fell to the floor. Maren let out a yelp, her eyes darting to the real ballerina, who got up, unharmed, with a ferocious expression on her angular face.

"I shattered my entire knee," whispered Obscura. "It took a year of surgeries and therapy to recover, and when I came back, the ballet director had given away all of my roles. He said my career was over, and I was a has-been." Obscura spit the words out like they were poison.

"So what did you do?" Maren asked.

"I came back to Rockpool Bay and met your darling sister."

Met. Like it was just a casual encounter, not a premeditated, evil scheme. Maren swallowed down the bitter retort on her tongue.

"Then I found my brother and paid him back for what he did to me."

A shadow man appeared on the screen. He stretched his arms and yawned, then climbed into bed. A shadow moth flitted over his head and dropped a gleaming dot into his mouth. In the corner of the screen, shadow Obscura crouched, watching. The shadow man jerked upright and silently screamed.

"After two weeks, he was too afraid to leave his house and go to work. Then he was too scared of his wife to leave his room." Shadow Obscura lunged and whirled and tossed handfuls of tiny dream sachets that sparkled on the screen. "I hunted down all of his old friends, too. And when people started leaving town, I realized the wonderful opportunity I had to remake this place in my own image."

Maren had been bullied half her life, but she'd never considered taking it out on everyone in her school, let alone the whole town. There was no excuse for that level of destruction. In one swift, silent move, she reached again, and this time her fingers slid over something metallic. A water bottle. She twisted her chair sideways by a fraction and dug her fingers deeper, through knitted fabric and extra pointe shoes. The phones had to be there somewhere. And maybe the EpiPen.

"I'm getting rid of all the magic in Rockpool Bay," said Obscura. "And now that I've got that whispering dust, I'm going to turn this place into something better. Something darker. People are going to respect *my* kind of magic, and they'll come to this theater every night to watch *me* dance. They'll hang on my every word. They'll bring me gifts.

They'll do whatever I say. Finally, everyone is going to adore and worship *me*."

Shadow moths flitted off the screen's edge and flapped across the backdrop. They scuttled across the floor, getting closer and closer to Maren's feet. She knew they were just illusions, but she hated the thought of them touching her. Giving her shoulder a hard twist, she shoved her hand deep inside the bag, and her fingernail grazed the rubbery edge of something. Her phone case. She'd held it so often that it felt like an extension of her hand.

Obscura came to a halt with a hungry glint in her eyes, and Maren snatched her hand back, but she held tightly to the mental image of the phone's exact spot inside the bag.

"Who will you give the whispering dust to?" Maren asked, wincing as shadow moths darted over her shoes. She swore she could feel their feathery wings brushing her ankles.

"Anyone. Everyone." Obscura's shadow whirled and leapt. "Imagine who I can control. Imagine what I can make them think, now that I've got my very own personal dream-maker."

"I'm not your personal dream-maker," muttered Maren. But she was already making the dreams. She didn't know how else to keep Lishta and Amos safe.

Maren watched closely as the ballerina jumped in and out of the beam of light, catching the shadow moths in her hands and tossing them into the air. She visualized the phone, nestled under something woolen in the far corner of the duffel bag. As Obscura swung into a dizzying quadruple pirouette, she lunged, jammed her outstretched fingers deep into the bag, and closed them around her cell phone.

"VOUS PUEZ COMME UN CHOU POURRI."

A screeching bird-voice reverberated through the empty theater. Maren's chair leg lifted off the ground and she tipped backward, suspended for a long, sickening moment, before managing to right herself and shove the phone under her thigh. Obscura stopped, midturn, and jogged over to turn off the projector. As the shadows disappeared, a bloodcurdling squawk filled the auditorium, and understanding dawned on the tall dancer's face.

"Is that the bird from your shop?"

Maren winced. As if this day weren't awful enough, here was Henri.

Obscura cocked her head. "I smell like a rotten cabbage?" she called. "Why don't you come say that to my face, you little feather duster?"

A feathery gray shape whirred down from the balcony and came to rest on the ballet barre. Henri cocked his head to the side, gave a trilling whistle, and croaked, "JOLIE MADEMOISELLE. BONJOUR, BONJOUR, CHERIE."

Obscura smirked. "Come to rescue your humans, have you?"

Henri hopped closer to Obscura and bobbed his head. "JOLIE, JOLIE," he chirped. Then he cocked his head toward Maren, lowered his voice, and let out a burst of rapid French. Maren squirmed in her chair as Obscura gave a delighted laugh.

"You're a vile little thing, aren't you?" She clicked her tongue and held out her arm, and without a second's hesitation, the traitorous bird flew straight to her wrist. Every mean thought Maren ever had about Henri was suddenly validated. She had a few more mean thoughts as she slid the phone out from under her leg.

Obscura drifted across the stage on her toes, with Henri perched on her shoulder. "I wonder if I could train you to deliver nightmares, too," she mused. Henri flapped his wings to maintain his balance as she twirled.

"Watch out," said Maren. "He loves to eat moths."

Obscura startled at that. While the ballerina made sure Henri didn't have his eye on the moth-bee in her hair, Maren turned her body and crossed one leg over the other so that it shielded the phone. She swiped her finger over the screen and pulled up the keypad.

9-1-

"Is something wrong with your chair?"

Maren slammed her leg down over the phone as Obscura strode toward her. "No," she squeaked. "It was just…sticky."

"Why are you in my seat, anyway?" Obscura kicked the duffel bag away, destroying Maren's chance of dropping the phone back inside.

"It was easier to reach things from here?" Maren's voice had gone up about three guilty octaves, and she hadn't meant to phrase it like a question.

Obscura pulled Henri from her arm and threw him into the air. With an outraged screech, he flapped, recovered, and flew away to the balcony. "Get up," she said.

Maren planted both her feet, as if she could somehow glue her legs and the phone to the chair. "I'm not done making this dream."

"I. Said. Get. Up." Obscura's moth-bee hummed into the back of Maren's head. Clutching the phone to her leg, Maren tried to swivel away, but as soon as she rose from her chair, Obscura grabbed her elbow. The phone flew out of her hand and hit the floor with a rubbery thunk. Shame flooded Maren's entire body, even though trying to escape was nothing to be embarrassed about. The thing to be embarrassed about was being foolish enough to get caught.

And oh, she was caught.

With her battered pointe shoe, Obscura kicked the phone away, and Maren's last dreg of hope tumbled off the stage with it. Then she opened a brown bottle and poured a sweet-smelling liquid onto a rag.

"I'm sorry," Maren whispered to Lishta and Amos, and to herself, as Obscura crossed the stage.

The rag covered Maren's mouth, and she fell into blackness.

Twenty-Four

THE UNFURNISHED ROOM HAD NO doors or windows. Red
paint covered its walls and floor; it dripped from the ceiling in
a steady rhythm. In the far corner of the room lay a furry lump:
a black cat curled up with its face hidden.

Plop. A droplet of paint landed in Maren's hair.

Plop. A droplet fell on the cat in the corner, which lifted its
head and opened glowing red eyes with vertical slits for pupils.

"Nice kitty," said Maren, because she hoped it was. But
those glowing eyes told her it probably wasn't.

The cat got to its feet and stretched. Somehow, the
curled-up black shape on the floor remained. It shifted and
became another cat, which stood and stretched. Then another
cat, and another, and another.

Normally, Maren loved cats. But the room was so small

and there were at least twenty of them now, their eerie, bright eyes locked on hers. She edged backward, casting around for a door, a hole, some way out of this awful room, but there was only wet red paint everywhere she touched. Her feet left crooked prints on the sticky floor. More cats, and more, and more, all with those searing eyes. Suddenly, they all crouched and hissed, and Maren's heart went icy.

Plop went a droplet of paint, right in Maren's eye.

Plop went another droplet in her other eye.

She tried to wipe them clear, but all she could see was stinging red. The cats' hissing grew louder, and furry bodies began to weave around her ankles. Back and forth and higher, up her legs, their razor claws piercing her skin.

"Go away," she whispered, trying to pull them off, but their fur was slick with paint. "Get off!"

The cats clambered up her back and chest, and a furry face rubbed against her cheek. Its breath drifted into her nostrils, reeking of rubber and rust and rot.

Maren screamed.

And woke.

But she couldn't open her eyes. She tried and tried for a long time before realizing they were already open, but it was so dark that it made no difference. Her head felt like a cracked egg, and dust clung to her lips and eyelashes. Maren eased up to her elbow and waited for the horrible spinning to stop. It was so much harder to stabilize when she couldn't see anything, couldn't tell which way was exactly up.

"Hello?" Her voice came out scratchy and dust-coated. "Is anyone there?"

Silence. Then a *click clack click clack* over her head.

"All I wanted was a few dreams." Obscura's voice was muffled, but her tone was sour and flat. "You didn't have to make me do that."

Panicky bile rose up Maren's throat. "Where am I?"

"Under the stage, where the trapdoors go." Obscura's shoes tapped closer. "It's called the trap room." She laughed like she'd just made a hilarious joke, and Maren bit her tongue to keep from screaming. "A few days in there should make you a bit more cooperative."

Something skittered past Maren, either a small rodent or a large bug. She scooted in the other direction, and her shoulder slammed into a hunk of metal. Overhead she could just make out a single line of grayish light, not bright enough to help her see anything.

"Where did you get that nightmare?" said Maren. Lishta had no dreams like that in her shop, and Maren had never heard of Hallie making one about cats. She had to admit, it was very good.

"I made it," said Obscura. "I held that jar of dream crystals under Gran-Gran's nose while she slept."

"You made…" Maren caught herself. If she told Obscura the truth, that the dream had been genuinely terrifying, Obscura might decide she didn't need to keep her around anymore. "I mean, of course you did," Maren said. "That makes perfect sense."

"Why?" snapped Obscura.

"Well, you did a good job…for a beginner." Maren layered false kindness over her words and tucked her feet up so nothing could crawl on them. "But the walls had a lot of patches with nothing on them, and every so often the cats turned into pencils."

Dead silence.

"But like I said, it was a really solid first attempt," added Maren quickly. "I screamed. Did you hear me?"

"I did." Obscura's voice was sharp and annoyed.

"A good nightmare is a work of art." Maren paused to consider her words. "It takes a lot of practice before you can craft something truly spectacular. You have to build up your… technique."

Another long pause. Maren brushed a strand of hair from her cheek and realized it was a cobweb. She slapped at her face, shook out her hair, and combed through it with her fingers, shuddering.

"I'll think about it," said Obscura.

The dark was so thick, Maren felt like it was eating her. "Could I please have a flashlight?"

The shoes click-clacked away.

"Please?" called Maren.

"I've got dreams to deliver," said Obscura's faint voice. "See you tomorrow…maybe."

"No!" Maren leapt to her feet. On tiptoe, she reached up until she felt splintery wood, the hinges and the edge of a trapdoor where the line of gray light glowed faintly. She pushed, but the door didn't budge. "Please! Don't leave me in here all night. I'll make any dreams you want. I promise I won't try anything funny. You can sit with me the whole time. I promise, I *promise*."

From somewhere in the distance came Obscura's voice, sharp and annoyed. For a second, Maren thought she was coming back to let her out, but then another voice joined in. A man's. Maren struggled to make out the words, but she recognized the slithering voice. It sounded like a centipede.

"I told you not to come here," yelled Obscura, and the man murmured and pleaded. Maren held her breath and tried to hear the rest of the conversation, but she only made out a few words: garbage cans and moths and midnight and something about a bribe, which caused Obscura to yell again and the man to apologize again.

Then Obscura's click-clacking shoes faded away. A door banged, and all went silent.

Maren sank to the gritty floor, tucked her knees up, and hugged them tight. She'd been right about Obscura being that man's business associate. She wondered how much he knew about her scheme, if he even knew Maren was here, locked in this awful, claustrophobic space that was surely swarming with spiders. Black spiders with long legs. Hairy, fat brown spiders. Jumping spiders. Maren stifled a sob.

"Mom," she whispered. "Dad, please come and find me."

Slowly, the line of gray overhead dimmed until it disappeared. Maren wished with every molecule of herself for a time machine. She'd go back to the moment where she and Amos found the note in the dream shop, and she'd call her parents instead of rushing to rescue Lishta. She'd go back further than that and tell Lishta the truth as soon as Obscura started threatening her. She'd go back further and never give Hallie that dream. Even further and tell Hallie to be careful at the traffic light.

It's all your fault, all your fault every step of the way, whispered a nasty voice in Maren's head. Because of her, Hallie was in a coma, and Lishta and Amos might as well be, too. If the police couldn't find them, Lishta might die and Amos's parents would lose their oldest son because of his kindness.

And Maren's parents would lose both of their daughters in the space of one summer. She'd watched her mother trying to make breakfast after the accident, burning egg after egg until they had no more left. She'd listened to her father crying in the shower sometimes when he thought nobody could hear. And now Maren was about to double their sorrow. Multiply it by a thousand.

All she wanted in the world was to go back, back, and curl up on the sofa with her mother, feel her arms around her, the soft cushion of her body, and her slow, deep breathing. She wanted her dad to come home and pretend he wasn't tired and make goofy jokes. She wanted to be warm and safe and loved.

And she wanted her sister. Maren imagined Hallie marching up to Obscura, disarming her with an elaborate tae kwon do move, and tying her up in a chair. Then they'd call the police and their faces would be all over the news. *Sisters Fight Off Kidnapper*. The articles would rave about how courageous the two girls were, how fierce and strong. But Maren wasn't strong enough to fight Obscura alone. As the ballerina kept pointing out, she was small and foolish and weak. No match for a grown-up. Not even brave enough to tell her grandmother the truth about what she'd done.

Maren buried her teary face in her arms, and her breath came in shuddering gulps. She let the dusty darkness swallow her for a long, long time, until her lungs ached and her tears had all been spent. There was nothing to hope for tonight. Everybody still thought she was staying at Lishta's.

And Hallie was moving in six days. There was nobody to cure her now. If Maren didn't figure out how to escape, her parents would bring her sister to the long-term facility on Friday, wondering the whole time what had happened to her.

It was all too much to think about. A cold numbness settled in Maren's bones as she let her eyes drift shut.

A tiny thump overhead.

Maren's eyes flew open.

"TA MERE EST UNE VACHE PARESSEUSE."

She staggered around, reaching blindly into the darkness, until she found a heavy block covered in dust and sticky, trailing threads. Trying not to think about the spiders involved, Maren dragged the block over to the approximate location of the trapdoor. It took a few minutes of shuffling and dragging and readjusting before she found the hinges again and pressed her mouth to the crack.

"Henri?" she said. "Are you there?"

Silence.

"Henri?"

An eardrum-bursting shriek flew down through the crack, and Maren wobbled on her block.

"Hey," she whispered. "You don't have to scream."

"TETE DE FROMAGE," said Henri.

"Listen," said Maren. "You need to go for help. Find a police officer or my parents. Say Maren is in the Starlight Theater. Say it, Henri. Maren is in the Starlight Theater."

Henri whistled, and his hopping sounds moved away across the stage.

"Henri!" commanded Maren. "Say it. Maren is in the Starlight Theater."

"MAREN IS," croaked Henri.

"Yes! Yes! Good bird. Maren is in the Starlight Theater. Maren is—"

"MAREN IS PLUS LAIDE QU'UN PHACOCHERE."

Maren let out a string of curses. "Maren is in the Starlight Theater, Henri. I swear, if you say this, I will buy you a lifetime supply of safety pins when I get out of here. Maren is in the Starlight Theater."

"MAREN IS IN THE STAR WITH PETER."

Maren felt sure Henri was laughing at her. "Star-*light* Theater. Star-*light* Theater."

"STAR TIGHT NEATER. CHAR BITE TWEETER. MAREN IS A BAR FIGHT CHEATER."

Even if he got it right, Maren realized, Henri had no idea what a police officer looked like or how to find her parents.

He'd never been out of the shop before, let alone to her house. Maybe once word got out that she'd gone missing, though, if he flew around town saying it, somebody would hear and understand.

Henri screeched into the crack again, and Maren cringed. "MAREN IS A STAR FART SKEETER."

The sound of his flapping wings faded. Then, from a long way away, "MAREN IS IN THE STARLIGHT THEATER."

It was a start. Now she had to get him out of the theater, but that wasn't going to happen tonight. Maren dragged her block over to a corner, pulled her jacket over her head to keep out the spiders, and got ready to wait out the night. Henri had given her a tiny ember of hope, just enough of a glow to keep her warm. She might not be big or strong enough to escape, but maybe she was smart enough.

Twenty-Five

SHE WOKE TO THE TASTE of oily fabric on her lips and feathery feet on her chin. With a yelp, Maren sat up, swatting at her face and spitting. Her jacket had fallen off, and something fluttered around her head.

"Get away!" She flapped her jacket in the moth's direction, but as soon as she stopped, it returned, brushing the back of her hair. She tumbled off the block and rolled away, hoping to evade the insect, but it could see better than she could in the dark, and within seconds it came back. Somewhere in the black depths to her left, Maren heard another quiet flitting sound. She strained for the sound of buzzing, but these seemed to be regular moths, rather than killer moth-bees, which was a small blessing at least.

Waving her hands blindly in front of her, Maren shuffled

in the opposite direction. Paper slid and small objects rolled under her feet. She hit something big and round and metal—a wheel of some sort, or a gear. Its rusty edge bit into her palm. With a hiss, Maren wiped the blood on her jeans and crept around the massive object. Her knee found a chair; her hands brushed over damp, moldy fabric, and she had no idea of the shape of the room around her, whether she was about to step into a hole or through a rotten floorboard. Behind her, the moths fluttered and searched, and she had to keep moving.

The floor sloped downward, its surface less cluttered as she went, but slick with moisture. The sour reek of mildew and old things filled her sinuses. Then she hit a crumbling cement wall. Maren walked her fingertips along it to the right, where she found a corner and more blank wall, then to the left, where she found the same thing. A dead end. No door, no window, no way out.

In the blackness, insect wings whispered. Maren clamped her mouth shut and dropped to her knees, brushing her hands across the slippery floor. There had to be something here: if not a way out, a weapon or a tool she could use to pry open the trapdoor leading to the stage. Assuming she could find her way back. Crawling feet landed on her head, and with a muffled shriek, she slapped at the moth, not caring if she crushed it into her hair. But it disappeared into the dark.

A few yards away, the floor glowed faint orange-yellow in a grid pattern. Maren ran to the glowing grid, which turned out to be a grate. A moth landed on her shoulder and she swatted it away. Another dropped onto her back, and Maren dug her fingers into the gaps between the metal and pulled. The sharp edges ripped at her skin, but she kept pulling, pulling, pulling. Finally, it gave way, and she tumbled backward. The grate clanged to the floor, and Maren froze, listening. Not daring to breathe.

Silence, except for the searching, flitting moths.

Maren squeezed through the hole backward, but the drop to the floor below was at least ten feet. Swiping a moth off her forehead, she braced herself on her elbows and reached back with her toes for a wall or a ladder, but found nothing.

Spindly moth legs tickled Maren's ear, but she couldn't get the insect off without losing her grip on the edge of the hole. Another landed on her nose. Maren whipped her head sideways.

GET OFF, she screamed inside her head, afraid to open her mouth. But the moth stayed fast. It tiptoed down over her upper lip, dragging something small and light. Maren caught a whiff of oil and metal and rot. A nightmare. She dropped her face to her shoulder, trying to smash it off.

Her elbows slid out from under her, and she fell.

Twenty-Six

MAREN HIT THE GROUND WITH a painful thump. She'd landed on a dirt floor in a long, empty room. On the opposite wall a battery-powered light glowed, casting everything in eerie shadows. Behind Maren, a set of metal rungs ran up the wall to the hole she'd fallen through. If she'd just reached back a little farther with her legs, she might have caught them. But it didn't matter—she'd made it down and nothing was broken, though her ankles and wrists ached from the impact.

In the center of the dirt floor lay a big metal shovel, perfect for digging a grave. Maren's teeth began to chatter as she pulled the battery-powered light off the wall. Easing a tarnished door open, she found a dark hall. It took her a moment to recognize it; she'd come down the other end with

Obscura the day before. She checked to make sure nobody was there, then crept to a door on the left.

"Gran-Gran?" Maren tried the handle, but it held firm. She racked her brain for some way to smash the door open, then remembered Lishta's hairpin in her pocket. The old lock yielded to her hairpin-rummaging in a couple of minutes. Maren threw open the door and ran to her grandmother's bedside.

"Gran-Gran, wake up!" she called, over and over, shaking Lishta, but the sleeping woman's mouth hung open as she snored. Obscura must have given her another dose of sleeping medicine. Maren tried to console herself with the fact that Obscura had used Lishta's breath on the dreamsalt, so she was still useful to keep alive.

"Gran-Gran!" she yelled once more.

"Maren?" A sleepy voice came from the room next door. Then a clank and a thump.

Maren dashed to Amos's door. His lock took longer to pick, but eventually the door opened. Amos sat on the floor, rumpled and filthy. As she stepped into the room, he scrambled backward, hitting his head on the corner of the bed.

"Are you okay?" said Maren.

A pause.

"Why do you even want to know?" mumbled Amos.

Maren stopped. "Why wouldn't I want to know if you're all right? Are you?"

Amos squinted at her and scoffed.

"What's the matter with you?" said Maren.

"I don't get it." The heaviness disappeared from his voice, replaced by biting anger. "I said I was sorry for all that Curtis stuff. I thought you were okay with it. I thought we were friends again."

"We are," said Maren. "What are you talking about?"

"This isn't funny anymore." To Maren's horror, Amos wiped tears from his eyes. "My mom's probably having a heart attack, looking for me."

Then it clicked. Maren edged closer. "Amos, do you think I locked you down here?"

Amos swore under his breath, and Maren sagged against the moldy wall. "Obscura has been feeding you whispering dust."

"Whispering *what?*"

"Dust. She's telling you things while you're asleep. Lying to you."

Amos shook his head like he wanted to clear it, and Maren sighed. "Think about it. Do you remember me actually putting you in that room?"

"I don't know. Everything's all jumbled up in my head." Amos's voice broke. "I don't even know if this is real right now."

"It is real. But I didn't put you in here. Obscura did. And then she fed you a kind of mind-control potion and told you it was me." Maren couldn't hide the fury in her voice. "You have to trust me, even though you probably don't want to."

Amos rubbed his eyes hard and stared at the floor. "I…do trust you. I'm starting to remember. Give me a minute."

Maren's foot tapped. She didn't really have a minute, but Amos needed time to put his thoughts in order. He rubbed his eyes again and took a few slow breaths.

"Okay," he said. "I *think* I remember you locking me down here, but I also remember the story you told me on the bus. I'm going to choose what to believe right now, and I choose you."

Maren swallowed the lump in her throat. "I need to find a way out of here. Will you help me?"

Unsteadily, Amos got to his feet and nodded. "Let's go."

⌒

The thought of leaving Lishta in this basement, even just until she could escape and get to the police station, made Maren ill, but she and Amos couldn't carry her while they searched for an exit. If Obscura returned, they'd have to run, either out of the theater or back to their rooms, and there was no way to do that while lugging a sleeping grandmother. Maren checked down both ends of the hall one more time, and then they slipped out of Amos's room.

"I'm starving," he said, and Maren's stomach grumbled in response. They snuck up the stairs to the stage and dug through the bins for anything edible, but there wasn't much: a handful of mint leaves, a cinnamon gumdrop, a few broken saltine crackers.

"I think we came in that way." Maren said, pointing to the back of the auditorium. "Let's see if the door is still open."

As they stole up the dark auditorium's sloping aisle, she listened closely for Henri, but he was either hiding or sleeping. Maybe he'd found a way out, though she hoped he hadn't, because the seed of a new idea had sprouted in her head and was beginning to grow. A backup plan, in case they couldn't get out.

Maren had no idea what time it was, where Obscura had gone, or whether that centipede man had left. She prayed they wouldn't run into either of them coming back in through one of the exits, though maybe if they did, she could distract them long enough to let Amos escape.

Light glowed through the gap between the doors at the back of the theater. Maren took a deep breath and beckoned to Amos. As she eased the door open, it made an awful, wrenching creak that brought tears to her eyes, but the lobby was empty. A string of blue battery-powered Christmas lights wound down the railing of a grand set of stairs. The once-elaborate carpeting lay in tatters, and the ticket windows were cloudy with dust and dirt. A smashed-up snack bar cowered in the corner like it was waiting for somebody to come back with a baseball bat and finish the job.

Amos leapt down the stairs and galloped toward the middle set of doors, slamming into them with a crash. They didn't budge, and pulling on them did nothing, either. Maren tried the other sets of doors, with the same useless result.

There had to be another way out.

"I am soooo hungry," moaned Amos as they passed the snack bar. Maren slipped behind the battered countertop and rummaged through shelves and cabinets, but all of the candy boxes had been gnawed on by mice.

"Milk Duds?" Amos held up a tattered package.

Maren considered it, then shook her head. "I don't think getting the plague is worth it."

He shrugged and stuffed a wad of stuck-together caramels into his mouth. Seconds later, his eyes bulged, and he spat the sticky lump onto the floor.

Mare rolled her eyes and pointed back toward the auditorium. "Let's follow all the exit signs. One of them has to be open."

But each door they found had been bolted shut, each window boarded up tight.

"Wow, she really planned this whole thing out carefully," said Amos, kicking an unyielding steel door.

Maren cringed, wondering how long Obscura had been planning this kidnapping, whether she'd planned to snatch Hallie first. She wondered how this all might have gone if she'd just warned Hallie and the car accident hadn't happened. It might have been Hallie trapped in this theater instead of her. Hallie probably would have figured out how to escape in five minutes flat.

Amos slipped into the stairwell that led to the basement, then poked his head out. "The stairs go up, too. Maybe there's a fire escape or window we can break and jump out."

"Good idea." As Maren followed him up the steps, a faint rustling sound grew louder. Delicate like the whispers of a thousand people all at once. Moths. Maren's skin went prickly as they reached the top and stepped into a hall filled with junk and shadows.

The moths' whispers grew louder until they were almost a roar, coming from behind a door on the right. Thousands of them, from the sound of it, fluttering and flitting and brushing against the other side. It might have been Maren's imagination, but the wood seemed to bulge with the weight of them.

"It's extra creepy up here," said Amos, zipping his sweatshirt up to his chin and stuffing his hands in his pockets.

"Cover your mouth," said Maren, pulling on her hood and tugging her shirt up over her nose. Amos did the same, and they tiptoed past the door. If they absolutely had to, Maren thought, they could check in that room for a window. After they'd exhausted all the other possibilities.

The next door opened onto a closet full of brooms and mops and cleaning products from another era. Before she left, Maren opened a container of bleach—so old it didn't have a childproof top—and tucked the cap into her pocket. The sprouting backup plan in her head had grown leaves and buds and was almost ready to bloom.

The door at the end of the hall had been left partially open, and a faint whiff of jasmine tickled Maren's nostrils. For all she knew, Obscura had returned hours ago and gone to sleep in this very room. But of all the places in the theater, Obscura's room was the most likely to have a window that opened and they couldn't pass up the chance. She crept closer, straining for the sounds of breathing, of movement, and pressed her face to the crack in the door.

The room was lit with the same blue Christmas lights as the lobby, and Maren could make out an antique fainting couch draped in gauzy scarves. She eased the door open a little further. A dressing table sat before a mirror. Still no Obscura. Holding her breath, Maren swung the door all the way open.

"VOUS PUEZ COMME UNE BANDE DE VIEUX PIRATES."

Amos screamed, and Maren's heart nearly flew out of her chest. Perched atop a lamp, Henri preened his tail feathers, clearly laughing at them. On the floor lay rows and rows of pointe shoes, their ribbons wrapped neatly around their heels, and an open sewing box. The window had been boarded up, just like all the others, and Maren wondered how Obscura could stand all the mildew.

"What are you doing in here, Henri?" she said.

"Apparently he's lurking around telling people they stink like old pirates," muttered Amos, jamming his shoulder into the unmoving window.

Henri flapped over to the dressing table and let out a gloppy white dropping before hopping onto a pile of papers. Maren nudged him out of the way and picked up the notebook on top. Inside she found a list of names, with Ernesto Perez at the top, followed by Maisie Mae and Mark Zottery, whose name had been crossed out. A line of check marks marched across the page after their names. Maren flipped through the next few pages, which were covered in hundreds of other names, many of which she recognized from town. Only a few had check marks after them, but Maren knew the rest were just waiting for Obscura to give them nightmares.

Imagine who I can control. Imagine what I can make them think. The evil woman's words echoed in Maren's mind.

"Look at this." Amos opened a folder filled with blurry photocopies. "She's got info on the whole police department, everybody who works at the town hall and the mayor's office, the department of public works, the board of selectmen, even the school board."

Maren's stomach felt like it was full of caterpillars. She sifted through the pile and found architectural plans for a massive, ornate theater, as well as for shops and restaurants and cafes. Even a school building. Maren couldn't begin to imagine what kind of school Obscura would run, how she'd force the kids to behave.

"Whoa." Amos pulled a black poster from underneath the bed. Silver designs of moths and thorny vines lined its borders, and in elegant silver script, it read:

The Shadow Theater
Featuring the Exquisite Obscura
Grand Gala Opening
January 5 at 7 p.m.
Attendance Is Mandatory

January was less than six months away. Maren had no idea how Obscura would manage to renovate the whole theater by then, but she also had no idea how she herself would survive six months in the woman's clutches if nobody came to rescue her. And there was no way Lishta could live that long asleep. Maren's hands went cold as she replaced the papers in the pile.

Somewhere downstairs, a door slammed.

"JOLIE MADEMOISELLE, JOLIE, JOLIE," yelled Henri.

Maren's chest seized up. "We need to get back to our rooms," she whispered. "So she won't know we figured out how to escape."

Amos started to protest, but she stuck her finger in his face. "I have a backup plan. Trust me."

He sighed. "Okay. But I really hate that room."

"Me too." Maren made sure the rows of pointe shoes were straight, then crept toward the door. "Don't you say anything about us," she warned Henri, but the bird was busy poking around in the sewing box, probably looking for safety pins.

Maren scooped up a length of satin ribbon and stuck it in her pocket with the bleach cap. Then she and Amos raced through the hallway and down the stairs to the basement, where she locked him back in his cell. Maren blew Lishta's door a kiss, then dashed into the room where the ominous shovel lay. She climbed the rungs on the wall and hoisted herself up through the hole.

After she had replaced the grate, Maren sat very still until wings fluttered beside her face. She swallowed her revulsion and let the insect crawl along her cheek to her mouth. As its tickly legs pressed at her lips, she caught the moth and crushed it in her hand, cringing at the papery crunch and the squish.

It was time to make her plan a reality.

Twenty-Seven

IT WAS MIDAFTERNOON, AND EVER since Obscura had returned and pulled her up through the trapdoor, Maren had been making dream after dream after dream. Apparently the wicked ballerina didn't require sleep, or even rest. She'd taken Amos out of his cell and put him to work sweeping up trash with his leg chained to a row of seats too far away from Maren for them to communicate. Then she had stretched, rehearsed, and fiddled with the projector for a few hours, changing the cutout puppets and experimenting with different-colored lights for the background.

Finally, she stopped long enough to eat a yogurt and a salad in a plastic takeout container. The enormous striped moth-bee flitted to the handle of her fork.

"Keep working," she snapped at Maren, who had never

felt such deep longing for a bite of raw kale in her life. But Maren had been busy on a little side project, in addition to the nightmares she was making. Unlike the black nightmares, this project came in a pink sachet. She also had a shiny silver safety pin tucked in her pocket.

All afternoon, Maren had been adding ingredients to the pink sachet, a pinch at a time whenever Obscura was too busy to notice. The second hand of a watch, a chip of paint from the piano in the orchestra pit, a scraping from the bleach bottle cap, a thread from Obscura's pointe shoe ribbons, a rabbit's toenail, and the legs of the moth that had been unlucky enough to try crawling into Maren's mouth. And thirty grains of dreamsalt, enough to keep a grown man asleep for two days. There was just one ingredient left to add, whispering dust, but Obscura had tucked the jar inside her duffel bag, which sat at the opposite end of the stage.

Paradiddle paradiddle heel toe heel, went Maren's feet.

Obscura snapped her empty salad container shut and ambled over to Maren's table. "Let me see what you've made," she said.

Maren pointed to the piles of nightmares, and Obscura gave them a satisfied nod. "You're much more cooperative than your sister. I should have tried you first."

Maren tugged so hard on her needle that the thread

broke. She needed to stay calm, keep moving forward with her plan, and not cause trouble.

"When I first started giving nightmares out, I wanted dreams about a wicked and beautiful dancer who lurked in the shadows." Obscura's dark eyes glittered. "I waited until Hallie was alone and I—" She let out a dainty cough. "Very kindly asked her to make some for me."

A black tunnel filled Maren's vision and grew until she could only see a tiny pinprick of the world.

"Alas, I made some foolish mistakes," continued Obscura. "I gave away a few too many details, and your sister started to figure out my game. She's much smarter than you. Correction: She *was* much smarter than you. That car crash was a lucky accident...for me."

Maren's urge to throw herself at Obscura and pummel her was unbearable. Instead she gripped the edges of the table and took ten, slow breaths. If she lost her temper, she'd ruin her plan. She glanced at the duffel bag and rearranged her expression into something close to a smile. "Did you use the whispering dust last night?"

"I did." Obscura swept to her barre and dropped into a lunge. "It's frightfully convenient how many people sleep with their windows open at this time of year. Just a pinch of dust on the sachets and my moths carried them in while I waited outside. I paid a visit to the police commissioner and told him there'd be a few things happening soon that he needn't trouble himself with investigating."

If Obscura used whisper dust on all of the police, there'd be nobody to help Maren. Or arrest Obscura, even if she managed to escape. There'd be nothing stopping Obscura from kidnapping Maren all over again. Maren fought the wave of panic rolling over her. Panicking never solved a problem.

"Then I stopped to see the owner of Stonemasters Construction," said Obscura. "Oh dear, I've forgotten his name again." She shrugged and swiveled her hips into a side lunge. "At any rate, he's woken up this morning with an overwhelming urge to rebuild this theater for free. And a sudden infatuation with a beautiful ballerina who rescued him in a dream."

Obscura's gloating grin made Maren want to vomit. "Who's that guy who was here last night?" she asked. "The one who's helping you open all those new businesses in town?"

The smug smile slid off Obscura's face. "How did you know about that?"

Using tweezers, Maren extracted a spider leg from a tiny jar. "I talked to him the other night outside the pharmacy."

"That's Cyril," said Obscura. "Did he tell you he was working for me?"

"Kind of." Maren slipped the spider leg inside a sachet.

He hadn't exactly, but it was better to let Obscura think her henchman was giving away secrets. "Where did he come from?"

"He grew up right here in Rockpool Bay," said Obscura. "Cyril has smoke magic. The ability to manipulate dirty, dark, *unhealthy* smoke. As you can imagine, he didn't feel very welcome in this town, either."

"Does he know we're here?" said Maren. "My grandmother and Amos and me, I mean."

"He knows what he needs to know," snapped Obscura.

I'll take that as a no, thought Maren.

"I found him waiting outside the stage door of a theater one night in Prague," said Obscura. "He recognized me from Rockpool Bay and had been following my tour for months before working up the courage to speak to me." The tall ballerina squared her shoulders. "Cyril does whatever I want, without needing nightmares or whispering dust. He doesn't quite have my level of…artistic vision, but he's rather clever at slipping into buildings, turning off freezers and replacing swarms of wasps in the Gree—"

"STARRRLIGHT THEATERRR."

A croaking bird shout boomed through the auditorium.

"MAREN IS IN THE STARLIGHT THEATER."

"What did he say?" Obscura peered out into the auditorium. Maren gripped the sides of the table and drew her breath in and out, in and out. *Shut up, Henri,* she thought with every fiber of her being.

"MAREN IS INNN…"

Muttering angrily, Obscura dumped a bin of dream ingredients onto the stage and began to rummage.

"Please, please don't say it again, Henri," whispered Maren.

"MAREN PARRRTRIDGE IS INNN THE STARRRLIGHT THEATERRR."

Obscura pulled a safety pin and a fist-sized chunk of concrete out of the clutter. Then she jumped into the orchestra pit and crept up the aisle. Amos dove behind a row of chairs.

"Henri," she called in a honeyed tone. "I've got a shiny new safety pin for you." She held the pin high overhead as she drifted through the rows of seats.

From the balcony came a greedy squawk.

"Pretty bird," she crooned. "Come get it."

"VOUS ETES VISQUEUSE COMME UNE ANGUILLE." Henri appeared on the balustrade. Obscura wound up like a baseball pitcher and hurled the chunk of concrete at him.

"No!" yelled Amos.

The bird let out a broken squawk and fell backward. A single gray feather floated down through the dusty air.

Maren choked on a sob. Henri was a member of her family, whether she liked it or not.

"Get back to work," barked Obscura. Maren's throat burned as she tucked the pink sachet under a strip of flowered wallpaper. Even with Henri gone, she couldn't bring herself to give up on this plan. Working on it had been the only thing keeping her from falling apart.

Obscura unlocked Amos's chain and led him onto the stage. As he passed Maren's table, he lifted his eyebrows and mouthed, *You okay?* Maren shrugged. Of course she wasn't. But she had to keep trying—there had to be another way to make this plan work.

Obscura stopped abruptly, and Amos almost walked into her, leaping back with a nervous yelp. The tall ballerina pulled the killer moth-bee off her shoulder and stood, muttering to herself and letting it crawl between her fingers.

"The whispering dust will work better if you put it inside the sachets instead of sprinkling it on top," squeaked Maren. "Do you want me to add it to some of them?"

Obscura's eyes were unfocused, almost like she'd forgotten Maren existed. Absently, she stuck the moth in her hair, then wiped her bleary eyes. "Tonight I'll have a chat with the president of the Rockpool Banking Trust and the school superintendent. They're about to have a budget surplus, and a sudden desire to build a new school—with a new headmistress." Obscura flashed a wicked smile, but the circles under her eyes had taken on a bluish hue. She was getting tired after all. "Cyril has some notes to type up and deliver, and I'll bring a little something over to Edna Frye, that bureaucratic cow. Then a quick stop at Cynthia O'Grady's and, last but not least, your lovely parents."

Maren's body went rigid at the mention of her parents and Amos's mother. She couldn't bear to think of the things Obscura might tell them, the devious ways she could make them forget about her or never want her to come home again.

"That's enough for one night." Obscura snapped her fingers like she was summoning a waiter. "Add the dust to six nightmares."

Maren made a show of considering all the piles of night-mares she'd made, then selected six at random and opened them up. "Can I have it, please?"

Obscura's pointe shoes dragged as she crossed the stage. From the duffel bag, she pulled the tin of whispering dust and held it out to Maren, but as Maren reached for it, she snapped it back.

"I'm not giving you the whole thing."

"Of…of course not," said Maren. "We just need a few grains for each sachet. I've got tweezers right here. Do you want to do it?"

Obscura stifled a yawn. "You do it. I'll watch to make sure you're not wasting it."

Maren eased the lid of the tin open and dipped her tweezers in. "This is just a suggestion," she said, "but you could give me, Amos, and my grandmother some of this dust when we're sleeping and make up a story about how we're all friends."

As she opened the tweezers over the first sachet, a few flecks of whispering dust fell onto the table. Maren pretended not to notice. "You could make us forget all about this whole kidnapping thing and take us back to the shop. You could also make us forget about the three-nightmare rule."

Obscura scowled and rubbed her mascara-crusted eyes.

"Then you could come in the store and ask us for a favor, and we could custom-make anything you wanted. Because we'd be friends, right? And then you wouldn't have to lock us up and...you know." Maren's hand shook as she added dust to the rest of the sachets and a bit more to the table.

Bzzzzzzzz.

Obscura's index finger, with the killer moth-bee perched on it, hovered inches from Maren's earlobe. Maren gulped and forced herself to hold statue-still.

"Doesn't sound like a very foolproof plan." Obscura turned away, dragging Amos with her.

"VOUS DANSEZ COMME UN HIPPOPOTAME."

The victorious croaking voice boomed through the theater. Maren never thought the day would come when she was thrilled to see Henri, but this was it. Her magnificent, implausible, only-option-left plan was still alive.

"That blasted bird." Obscura shielded her eyes and scanned the auditorium. Quickly, Maren scooped up the extra particles of whispering dust with a scrap of paper and tipped them inside the pink sachet.

"I think he's behind there." Amos pointed at a curtain on the other side of the stage, in the completely wrong direction, and flashed Maren a thumbs-up as Obscura stalked over, dragging him with her.

Maren sewed up the edge of the pink dream and tucked it into her sleeve. Moments later, Obscura returned with Amos and no bird. She checked her watch, then glared at Maren.

"I'm going to lie down for an hour. Get back in the trap room."

It was time.

As she crossed the stage, Maren let the pink dream slip out of her sleeve. She gave a quiet, pretend cry of dismay and crouched to scoop it up.

Obscura kicked the sachet away before Maren could take it. "What is that?"

"N-nothing." Maren added an extra quaver to her voice.

"Tell me."

Buzzing wings tickled Maren's eyebrow, and this time the quaver in her voice was real. "I made it for my sister to give her strength and energy and—" She snatched a glance at Obscura, whose tired eyes gleamed. "Power. The power to heal, that is. I was going to give it to her the other day at the hospital." Maren let all of the terror and stress and agony of the past two days pour out. Tears streamed down her cheeks, and even though she'd started out pretending, they were real. "Please, please don't get rid of it. I've never made anything so beautiful and potent in my life, and I just wanted her to have it."

With a smug grin, Obscura tucked the dream inside the pocket of her warm-up top, and the killer insect zapped away. A hysterical squeak of a laugh slipped out through Maren's tears, and she covered it with a sob as she climbed down into the trap room, not daring to look at Amos.

The wheels of her plan had creaked into motion.

Twenty-Eight

Maren waited until Obscura's footsteps faded away across the stage. Then she waited a bit longer. She silently marked out her routine for the tap-dancing recital four times, then every other combination she could think of, plus a few more she made up. The trap room felt no less creepy and stifling in the daytime, but at least there didn't seem to be any moths. She wiped her mouth and ran her fingers through her hair, just to be sure. Then she dragged the block underneath the trapdoor and pulled the safety pin from her pocket.

"Henri," she whisper-yelled, poking the pin up through the crack. "Look what I've got."

No answer. Maren stood on tiptoe and jammed the safety pin up so far that splinters dug into her fingers.

"Henri! Come get this beautiful, silvery safety pin. Here,

birdie-birdie." Her lips were so dry it took her several tries to manage a whistle.

Suddenly the safety pin jerked. Maren almost lost her grip, but managed to snatch it back. From the stage above came an irritated squawk.

"Henri." Maren poked just the tip of the safety pin up, not enough for him to get a grip on. "Can you say something new for me?"

Henri's beak scrabbled around, trying to get the pin.

"Henri," said Maren. "Say, 'You'll never, ever wake.'"

"MAREN IS IN THE STARLIGHT THEATER."

Maren wiggled the safety pin a little so that it would catch the light. "That's very good, but let's try this one: You'll never, ever wake. You'll never, ever wake. Say it, Henri."

"TON PERE EST UN HAMSTER."

"Listen to me, Henri," said Maren, determined not to let the frustration show in her voice. "This is to help Gran-Gran. You want to save her, don't you?"

A long pause.

"EVERRR WAKE."

"That's it!" Maren pushed the pin nearly all the way out and let Henri get a good taste of the metal, then drew it back. "You'll never, ever wake until you let them go."

"NEVERNEVER WAKE, YOU'LL NEVERNEVER WAKE."

"Good," whispered Maren. "You'll never, ever wake until you let them go."

"UNTIL YOU LET THEM GO. YOU'LL NEVER, NEVER WAKE."

Maren made him practice a few more times, then jerked the safety pin all the way inside. "Henri, listen to me."

The bird's clawed feet hopped one way, then the other.

"Henri, are you listening?"

Another earsplitting squawk.

"Henri, go find Obscura. The jolie mademoiselle. Go to that room with the lamp and find the jolie mademoiselle."

"JOLIE MADEMOISELLE. BONJOUR, BONJOUR, CHERIE."

"Yes, that's right." Maren's heart danced a cha-cha in her chest. "Go find her and say, 'You'll never, ever wake until you let them go.' Tell the jolie mademoiselle that, and then we'll be able to save Gran-Gran." Maren pushed the safety pin all the way up, and it left her fingers. "Hurry!"

"YOU'LL NEVER, NEVER, NEVER, NEVER WAKE." Henri's screech faded as he flapped away. "TES POCHES SONT PLEINES DE NOUILLES."

Exhausted, but fizzing with tiny bubbles of hope, Maren

dropped back down onto the dusty block. There was nothing to do now but wait.

Twenty-Nine

TWENTY MINUTES LATER, THE TRAPDOOR flew open. A slender hand reached into the gloom, and Maren took it. With surprising strength, Obscura hoisted her up and she tumbled onto the stage. The ballerina's eyes were closed—she was fully asleep—but she turned and ran to the back corner of the stage. She wore one untied pointe shoe, and the other foot was bare. With a yelp of fear, she began to leap across the stage, her feet flying ten times as fast as normal. She let out a tiny snore as she rounded the front of the stage, leapt over Maren, and waved frantically at the orchestra pit.

"Slow it down! I can't keep up," she panted as she lunged and whirled. "Somebody tell the conductor."

Biting her lip to keep from laughing, Maren stepped out

of the way. This was phase one of the nightmare she'd made. Henri had been successful in his mission.

"NEVER, EVER WAKE!" The parrot soared into the room, clutching a crushed and very dead killer moth-bee in his claws. He landed on the table and began munching on the insect.

"You wonderful, beautiful bird," whispered Maren.

"I did…let…her…go!" Obscura forced the words out between frenzied jumps. "Wait, what's happening?" She came to a screeching halt, then tapped her right foot. Then her left foot began to shuffle. "No one told me there was *tap* in this solo!" she wailed as her feet skipped faster and faster in a terrible, messy approximation of tap dancing.

This time Maren couldn't hold back her laughter. A thread from the stitching of an old tap shoe had been her secret ingredient. "Have you let Amos and Lishta go yet?" she said, forcing sternness into her voice.

The ribbons of Obscura's pointe shoe flapped as she kick-ball-changed. "I just need the conductor to slow down the music. I can't, I can't!"

"Where are your keys?" said Maren.

Obscura's hand went to a chain around her neck, but then she shook her head. "You can't have them."

"Well then, you'll never, ever wake," sang Maren, edging

closer. It was just about time for phase two of the nightmare. "Ooh, what's that in the wings?"

Obscura fell out of her turn and sprawled on the floor. Her foot jerked out from underneath her like something had pulled it.

"Let go of me!" she screamed. "Oh, oh no, it's got my ribbons." She jerked her foot, tugged on her knee with both hands, but the leg stayed out. Obscura covered her already-closed eyes, snored, and shuddered. "Nice bunny," she whispered. "Good bunny. Stay over there, please stay over there."

Maren had considered making the nightmare about a snake, but decided it was too cruel to give Obscura the same traumatic dream that had set her on this wretched path. Besides, she knew how to make plenty of other things scary. Even rabbits.

"He *loves* to play with ribbons," she said. "Look how sleek his fur is, how sharp his teeth are."

Obscura peeked through her fingers, though her eyes were still closed, and screamed. "Get it away!"

"Give me your keys," said Maren.

Obscura pulled off a long chain necklace with several keys on it and flung it in Maren's direction. Her head lolled forward, her chin resting on her chest, and she snored again.

"Stay here with her," Maren said to Henri as she snatched up the keys.

"JOLIE MADEMOISELLE! NEVER, NEVER WAKE!" The parrot perched on the edge of the trapdoor, munching on the striped moth.

"It's pinning you to the floor," Maren said to Obscura. "You can't move."

Obscura lay down flat on the stage, arms by her sides, whimpering and twitching.

As Maren flung open the door to the stairwell, a cloud of moths swept out. With a shriek, she jumped back, swatting and swiping. Obscura must have misunderstood Henri's instructions and let the moths go, too. They landed in her hair, they covered her sweatshirt, they crawled inside the cuffs of her sleeves and pants. They coated the walls of the stairwell and zoomed in from all directions. They zipped past Maren and into the theater, where they descended on the table, swooping in to snatch up nightmares. The moths were going rogue.

"Leave those alone!" yelled Maren, but she didn't have time to deal with them. Clamping one hand over her mouth and nose and shielding her eyes with the other, she ran into the stairwell and clattered down the stairs.

"It's me! I'm breaking you out!" she yelled to Amos,

swatting at her face as she tried each key in his lock and wondered if she should just use Lishta's hairpin again. Finally, the door swung open and Amos dashed out. Flailing and slapping away moths, they ran to Lishta's cell, unlocked it, and slammed the door behind them. Maren crushed three of the four moths that had managed to follow them inside. The last one fluttered up to the battery-powered light on the ceiling and began throwing itself at the plastic bulb.

"Gran-Gran." Maren dropped to her knees beside the old woman, whose face was sunken and slack. "Gran-Gran!" She shook her shoulder, but Lishta didn't respond. Panic crushed Maren's chest as she felt Lishta's wrist for a pulse. There it was, beating weakly under the papery skin. Maren held her finger under Lishta's nose. Little puffs of breath came out. Worryingly faint, but there.

"Gran-Gran, please wake up. Please, please, please." Maren shook her grandmother's shoulder, and Lishta's head lolled sideways as she let out a wispy sigh and murmured something about bat fur and tea.

"Let's carry her upstairs," said Maren.

"Are you sure?" Amos eyed the sleeping old woman dubiously.

Maren swatted another moth away. "We can't just leave her down here with all these nightmares flying around. And given how much dreamsalt I put in Obscura's dream, she'll be out cold for hours."

Amos helped her hoist Lishta out of bed, draping her arms over their shoulders. Even though the old woman was bird-light, they struggled to get her down the hall and then move her trailing feet up each step as the moths circled and swarmed.

"Watch out!" yelled Amos, jerking his head toward Lishta as he swung them around the banister of the landing.

A furry yellow moth carrying a black sachet landed on the old woman's chin. Maren slapped it off, but the insect stuck to her damp hand, and when she wiped it off the nightmare smeared across her palm.

Lishta's eyes fluttered, then she tipped suddenly backward and nearly sent them all tumbling down. Maren needed to clean her hand, but it was physically impossible while holding up her grandmother. A skeleton with long, stringy, black hair darted across the landing overhead. Already, the nightmare was taking effect.

"It's not real," muttered Maren. "It's not real."

Finally, they reached the top of the stairs, dragged Lishta into the wings, and propped her against the wall. Obscura lay unmoving on the stage, covered from head to toe in writh-ing, flapping, crawling moths. The sound of all those beating, whirring wings set Maren's teeth on edge. More insects zoomed in from the wings, but there was almost no space left on Obscura to land. A few remained in flight, circling the high ceiling of the auditorium.

As much as Maren detested the woman, it was hard to look at her under all those moths. Especially her face. Quickly, Maren turned toward the table, but the skeleton sat there, sewing up a dream with its bone fingers and watching her with empty eye sockets. Its greasy hair looked exactly like her Halloween witch wig from two years ago. She'd helped Lishta make this dream using strands from that wig, but that didn't make it any less scary.

"Not real, not real, not real," she whispered, then turned to Amos. "We need to make a waking antidote." She closed her eyes, trying to visualize all the ingredients. "Spearmint, dried firefly, lemon zest, and cayenne pepper. Oh, and coffee."

Amos helped her as she swept through the ingredients on the floor. Maren made sure not to touch the skeleton's foot, which tap-tap-tapped along to a high-pitched, creeping melody that she knew no one else could hear.

Once everything had been found except the firefly, which was probably still at the shop, Maren ground it up and took a pinch, not bothering to put it in a sachet. Amos held open Lishta's mouth while she pushed it under her tongue, praying that it would work, that an overdose of Obscura's sleeping medicine hadn't permanently damaged her grandmother's brain.

Moments later, Lishta stirred. She clawed at her mouth, but Maren took her hands gently away and held them.

"It's okay, Gran-Gran. It's not a nightmare. Just leave it there until you're all the way awake."

Lishta's eyes fluttered open, and her face burst into a radiant, wrinkly smile. "I'm so happy to see you, darling," she said. "And you," she said to Henri, who had landed on her shoulder and was busy combing her messy hair with his beak.

"I'm happy to see you, too." Maren's voice broke as she thought about everything they'd been through, everything that might have happened.

Amos had found the duffel bag and was already on the phone with the police, repeating their names and their location.

Maren squeezed her grandmother's hand tight. "It's all going to be okay now."

Thirty

MAREN SAT AT A TABLE in the storeroom, surrounded by all of the secondhand typewriters Lishta had bought over the past year but hadn't had time to clean and repair. In front of her lay a 1960s Remington Quiet-Riter model with its lid off and a rag tucked under the type-bars that swung forward and stamped the letters onto paper. The ink-crusted letter plates were called slugs, and Maren had always wondered where the name came from. They were nothing like the slimy creatures she found in her mother's garden and that Lishta sometimes dried and powdered for dreams.

Maren squirted cleaning solution into the typewriter's innards and dug in with her metal brush. This was the second part of her punishment for breaking Lishta's rules, in addition to being banned from the dream shop for a month.

Considering what should have been her punishment, it wasn't bad, even though the cleaning chemicals made her sneeze every few minutes and her fingernails were stained permanently black.

Shuffle ball change stamp shuffle ball change went Maren's feet under the table. *Stamp step stamp step.*

The door creaked open. Lishta pulled out the chair beside Maren and removed a dusty gray Smith Corona from its carrying case. "How did it go at the station?" she said, picking up a square of sandpaper and scrubbing at the V key.

"Not too bad." This was the second morning Maren had spent at the police station making various official statements. She'd answered the same questions over and over, so many times now that the horrible fear swirling in her chest whenever she thought of the Starlight Theater had been replaced by brain-numbing boredom.

The police hadn't found Cyril yet, but they assured her it was only a matter of time. All of the black and silver signs had disappeared from the town's businesses overnight. The Green and Fresh, Maisie Mae's, the pharmacy, and Beverly's tea stall had reopened, though the Zotterys loved New Zealand and wanted to stay there. The fortune-teller's tent remained on the boardwalk—apparently she had nothing to do with Obscura and Cyril's plot.

Business at the dream shop was booming. After word of Obscura's plot to take over the town had gotten out, loads of people were interested in buying nightmares. However, Lishta had decided to stop selling them—at least the truly frightening ones. She said she might consider selling dreams like the pyramid teddy bears in a few months, once all the hype died down.

"I was foolish to let that woman into the shop again." Lishta ground her sandpaper into the letter B. "But she was banging on the door all in a tizzy, yelling that something had happened to you."

Maren sneezed. "Amos said the only person we should be blaming is Obscura," she said. "It's really hard to do that, but I think he's right."

It was more of a hopeful question than a statement. Lishta dabbed a droplet of polish onto a rag. "He's a smart boy. But the next time an evil moth-wielding ballerina tries to blackmail you, you must promise to tell a grown-up."

The old woman's eyes sparkled, and Maren could almost see the humor in the situation now that it was over. Everything still felt a little bit empty without Hallie, and she still missed her old life, but this new life was much easier to appreciate now that she'd almost lost it. Maren scrubbed at the slugs of her typewriter, which slowly changed from black to silver, and she marveled at how wonderful it felt to have a full stomach and clean clothes and not be constantly afraid of dying.

"I have a proposal for you," said Lishta. "If you're willing to help me with some experiments, I might consider shortening the time of your ban from the dream shop."

"Yes!" Maren leapt up, knocking over a can of compressed air. "What?"

With a smile, Lishta reached into her apron pocket and pulled out the tin of whispering dust.

⁓

The next afternoon, Maren and Amos sat in old Mr. O'Grady's nursing home room, listening to the old man's wheezy snore.

"It should be done now." Maren checked her watch. Her dreams still weren't as precise as Lishta's, but she'd designed this memory to last somewhere between two and three minutes. Before Mr. O'Grady had consented to taking the dream, he seemed to recognize Amos but kept calling him "young man." Maren suspected he couldn't remember his name. She hoped that would change when he woke, but there was no knowing for sure. Her dreams couldn't work miracles.

"Gramps, can you hear me?" Gently, Amos shook the old man's shoulder.

Mr. O'Grady let out a sharp snort and lifted his head. His

unfocused gaze drifted around the room, and Maren worried they were too late and his brain had deteriorated beyond healing. But then he spotted his grandson and smiled.

"Amos, my boy!" he croaked. "I was just dreaming about playing softball with you."

Amos let out a surprised laugh, and Maren pretended not to notice the tears in his eyes. "I'll be right back," she said, easing out of her chair. "Just need a drink of water."

Out in the hall, Maren gulped and gulped from the water fountain until the world around her swam. She was thrilled to help Amos's grandfather remember him again, especially after everything Amos had done for her. Yesterday, she'd even gotten a sincere apology from Curtis, something she'd never imagined in her wildest dreams.

Maren sighed. Nothing made her happier than finding the perfect present for somebody else. But it had been so easy to heal Mr. O'Grady's brain, and she couldn't quite bury her own jealousy. As delighted as she was for Amos and his grandfather, she still felt sorry for herself and Hallie. She'd begun testing the whispering dust with Lishta, but that didn't change the hospital's no-magic policy, and Maren wasn't sure about the long-term facility's rules.

Tomorrow Hallie was moving to Whittaker. Everyone assured Maren it wouldn't change anything, but it changed everything. Her sister was going to that hopeless place. Maren had failed to fix her.

From inside her backpack came a melodic trill. She fished out her phone. "Hi Mom."

"Sweetie? Can you hear me?" Her mother sounded frantic, and Maren's stomach clenched.

"Yes. What's going on?"

"Your sister is awake!" yelled Maren's mom. "Completely, fully awake and responding to questions. She asked for you."

Maren let out a scream, startling the old people in the hall. "Sorry," she said to them. "It's good news, don't worry. Mom? Are you still there?"

"Yes. You're still at the nursing home, right? I'm almost there. Meet me outside."

Maren threw her phone into her bag, stuck her head into Amos's grandfather's room to tell them the good news, and ran for the exit.

~

Fifteen minutes later, Maren and her mother careened into the hospital parking lot, neither one of them having double-checked their seat belt or whispered self-affirmations at traffic lights. They swung into an empty spot beside Lishta's duct-tape-covered Beetle, and Maren flung herself out of the car before her mother had even shifted into park.

"Come on!" she yelled.

Laughing, they ran to the entrance. The glass doors swished open, and they slowed to a speed-walk, throwing a quick hello to the woman at the front desk. Up zoomed the elevator, not stopping until the fifth floor. Maren gave the ridiculously happy unicorn on the wall a double thumbs-up and thundered down the hall to her sister's room.

Lishta and Maren's dad sat on either side of Hallie's bed, holding her hands, and Henri hopped around the bedside table, shredding Kleenex with his beak.

As soon as Hallie caught sight of Maren, her face broke into a massive grin. "Hey, little sis," she said in a rusty voice.

"COCHON GROGNON. MAREN IS IN THE STARLIGHT—"

"Henri, I will put you *in the car*," warned Lishta. With an offended squawk, Henri flapped over to the windowsill, where he began preening his feathers. Lishta stood and gestured for Maren to sit in her chair.

Maren took Hallie's hand and squeezed, not too hard. Her heart was trying to tap-dance out of her chest. There were so many things she wanted to say, she didn't know where to start.

"How are you feeling?" she finally said.

"Okay," croaked Hallie.

Maren inched closer to her sister. Her beautiful, kind, wonderful sister who she'd thought might never speak to her again. Maren had never felt this kind of dazzling, dizzying happiness in her entire life.

"Do you remember anything I told you while you were asleep?" she said.

Hallie closed her eyes and nodded slightly.

"You did hear," said Maren, beaming. "Anyway, you don't have to worry about her anymore. Obscura… Ms. Malo is in jail now. The trial hasn't started yet, but considering all the evidence, the police don't think she'll be out for a very long time—if ever."

Eyes still closed, Hallie smiled. "Good," she mouthed soundlessly, then rolled onto her side and her hand went slack as her breathing slowed. Maren's mom crossed the room and stroked her hair.

"It's okay," she said to Maren. "The doctors said this is normal sleep now. Do you want to grab some lunch while she rests?"

Maren shook her head. "You go without me. I'll stay here."

After everyone had filed out to the cafeteria, she squeezed into the bed, resting her cheek against Hallie's back. Listening to the gentle rhythm of her sister's breath, Maren drifted off to sleep, too.

Thirty-One

MAREN STOOD IN THE WINGS of the Rockpool Bay Community Theater, dressed in an itchy red and gold sequined leotard and matching hat. Shivering a little, she watched the stage, where the level-four jazz class shimmied and sashayed in black fringed costumes. Counting dress rehearsal, this was the second time she'd been on a stage since those awful days in the Starlight Theater.

Today, she had nothing to worry about, other than forgetting the steps to the routine. Nobody was making mind-control nightmares or brandishing killer moth-bees. Maren's brain knew that, but her wobbling knees and flapping stomach didn't seem to have gotten the message. When she closed her eyes, she could almost feel that hideous insect's wings buzzing against the back of her head.

No.

She patted the hairnet holding her bun tight, adjusted a bobby pin on her hat, and shook out her legs, carefully keeping the taps on her shoes quiet. Obscura was locked away, Maren had outwitted her, and she had saved Lishta, Amos, and all of Rockpool Bay. She might not be big or strong, but she was smart and brave. And being brave meant ignoring the butterflies in her stomach and the phantom moth behind her head; it meant getting on that stage and moving forward with her life.

The stage lights blinked out as the level-four jazz class shuffled off the stage to loud applause. Maren's heart rocketed as the darkness closed around her, just like it had in the trap room under the Starlight Theater's stage. But then she spotted the glowing green tape that marked the various locations on the stage. The girls from her class filed out from the wings, and someone gave Maren's hand a quick squeeze.

She had this. She knew her steps. She was as ready as she'd ever be.

In the front row, a tiny red light shone. Her parents had gotten special permission to livestream Maren's performance so Hallie could watch it at Whittaker with Lishta. This was Maren's birthday present for her sister, and Hallie said it was utterly perfect. The doctors said she'd be ready to come home after just a few more weeks of physical therapy. Maren could wait a few more weeks.

"Love you, big sis," she whispered as she took her place in the second row, set one hand on her hip, and placed the other on the brim of her hat.

The lights beamed on, bounding off the sequins on seventeen dancers' costumes. A visual explosion of flashing, sparkling, scintillating red and gold.

Maren's smile shone brighter than all the sequins combined.

The music swelled, and her feet began to tap.

Acknowledgments

A massive, blue-whale-sized thank-you to my agent, Kathleen Rushall. I truly appreciate your encouragement, guidance, and persistence over the years. Thanks for always having my back, for bringing such positive energy to everything, and for nudging my ideas in just the right direction.

Thank you to my editor, Annie Berger, for all of your wisdom and guidance and for shaping this book into something I'm really proud of. Thank you to Cassie Gutman, Lynne Hartzer, and Susan Barnett for polishing this book and making it shine. Thank you to Federica Frenna for her gorgeous illustrations and to Jordan Kost and Danielle McNaughton for the wonderful design. Thanks also to Jackie Douglass, Caitlin Lawler, and the rest of the Sourcebooks team. I can't think of a better home for Maren!

Thank you to Margot Harrison for reading approximately nine thousand versions of my various books over the years and for being so kind and supportive. Thanks to Jesse Sutanto for always making me laugh and for crawling through the submission trenches with me. Thank you to Marley Teter for your friendship and your whip-smart notes.

Thank you to Addie Thorley, Candace Andersen, Gloria Mendez, and Sam Taylor for reading and giving such excellent feedback on my drafts.

Thank you to Tom Furrier, owner of Cambridge Typewriter, for running the super-cool, travel-back-in-time store that inspired Maren's dream shop. Readers, if you ever want to catch a whiff of that amazing typewriter smell and admire all the old machines, check this place out!

Thank you to my mother, Lynn, for filling our house with books, for all those trips to the library, and for nurturing a lifelong love of reading. Thank you for always believing in me, for telling me never to give up even when I was sure it was inevitable. This book literally would not exist without you. Thank you to my sister, Alissa, for cheering me on and cheering me up when I get grumpy and stressed. Thank you to my dad, Steve, the original Mr. Alfredo. I'm so sad you never got to see this book published, but you've been with me in spirit always.

Thank you to my husband, Ciaran, for always being there for me. For celebrating all the highs with me and hugging me through all the lows. Thank you to my children, Isla and Neil, for being wonderful human beings, for always making me laugh, and for the many fantastic ideas that made their way into this book.

Finally, thank you to my readers! I hope you enjoyed this story.